St Elizabe

Dealing with sick kids can be heartbreaking, funny, and uplifting, often all at once!

This series takes a look at a hospital set up especially to deal with such children, peeping behind the scenes into almost all the departments and clinics, exploring the problems and solutions of various diseases, while watching the staff fall helplessly in love—with the kids and with each other.

Enjoy!

Maggie Kingsley lives with her family in a remote cottage in the north of Scotland surrounded by sheep and deer. She is from a family with a strong medical tradition, and has enjoyed a varied career including lecturing and working for a major charity, but writing has always been her first love. When not writing, she combines working for an employment agency with her other interest, interior design.

Recent titles by the same author:

CHANGING LIVES

MAGGIE KINGSLEY

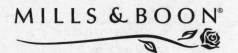

First published in Great Britain 2000
Harlequin Mills & Boon Limited,
Eton House, 18-24 Paradise Road, Richmond, Surrey TW9 1SR

© Maggie Kingsley 2000

ISBN 0 263 82435 7

Set in Times Roman 10½ on 11¼ pt.
112-0012-59143

Printed and bound in Spain
by Litografia Rosés S.A., Barcelona

Chapter One

IT WOULD have been a lot easier, Peggie decided afterwards, if she could have laid the blame on her Aunt Maeve's ample shoulders—a lot easier, but unfortunately not the truth.

Her aunt couldn't possibly have foreseen that the umbrella she'd bought her favourite niece for Christmas would blow itself inside out just as Peggie reached the imposing entrance of St Elizabeth's Children's Hospital. And she most definitely couldn't have predicted that when Peggie was desperately attempting to wrestle it back under control she would cannon straight into a tall, rain-coated figure, sending his briefcase flying into a very large and muddy puddle.

'Oh, I'm so sorry,' she gasped, abandoning her umbrella as a lost cause and reaching for the briefcase just as the man did the same.

'Not half as sorry as I am, believe me,' a deep Welsh voice groaned when their heads promptly collided.

For a second Peggie saw stars. For an even longer second she found herself gazing into a pair of the greenest eyes she'd ever seen, but when the man straightened up and gingerly ran his fingers over a head of hair so wet it could have been any colour, concern flooded through her.

'Are you all right?' she asked, peering anxiously up at him from under the hood of her ancient but still very serviceable duffle-coat. 'I'm a doctor—'

'So am I, but I can't say I've ever been so desperate for patients I've taken to assaulting people in the street in order to get them,' he interrupted tightly.

A faint tinge of colour appeared on her cheeks—a tinge

which darkened to crimson when she hurriedly retrieved his briefcase and held it out to him only to see a rivulet of dirty water splatter down from it onto his immaculate raincoat.

'Oh, I'm so sorry!' she cried in dismay as the man's eyes rolled heavenwards. 'I didn't realise—I didn't think—I should never have brought that wretched umbrella with me this morning but I didn't want to arrive here wet—'

'Here?' he broke in, his dark eyebrows snapping together. 'You're a doctor here—at Lizzie's?'

She nodded. 'I start tomorrow.'

'Your unsuspecting patients have my sympathy.'

She bit her lip and pulled a handkerchief from her pocket. 'It's only a little bit of muddy water,' she observed, reaching out to dab at the marks on his coat. 'I'm sure I can quite easily…'

'Can quite easily what?' he demanded as she came to a horrified halt, all too aware that instead of making the stains better she was, in fact, making them considerably worse.

She risked a quick glance up at him and her heart quailed. 'I—I was only trying to help,' she faltered. 'I'm so—'

'Sorry,' he completed for her caustically. 'Look, Dr Whatever-your-name-is, I'd be greatly obliged if you didn't try to help me any more. I don't think either my nerves or my clothes could stand it.'

'But—'

'There is one thing you can do for me, however.'

'Name it,' she exclaimed. 'I'll do anything.'

'Keep as far away as possible from me in future!' he snapped, before whirling round on his heel and striding into the hospital, leaving her staring unhappily after him, heedless of the biting March wind and heavily falling rain.

It hadn't been her fault, she told herself as she picked up her ruined umbrella and followed him. It had been an accident which could have happened to anyone. Well, perhaps not quite to anyone, she conceded as she crossed the hospital foyer and made her way towards the elevators. Who else did she know who could antagonise the very first member of staff they chanced to meet within seconds of arriving at a new hospital?

She wondered which department he worked in. Administration, judging by the weight of his briefcase, which meant that with luck she might never see him again. And she didn't want to see him again, she decided as she got into one of the elevators. He might have possessed a pair of the most stunning green eyes she'd ever seen but friendly he most certainly was not.

'Which floor, love?' the man who had followed her into the elevator asked as she let out a deep sigh.

'The second, please,' she murmured.

'The second?' he exclaimed, reaching past her to press the elevator button. 'Now, sure and begorra, I don't believe a lovely colleen like yourself can be wanting Plastic Surgery?'

Irritation flooded through her. Why did people always make fun of her Irish accent? The man she'd collided with earlier had possessed a very marked Welsh accent and she'd bet money nobody ever made fun of *him*.

Vexedly she turned, fully intending to give the man a piece of her mind, and blinked. With his thick blond hair, deep brown eyes and warm smile, he had to be quite the handsomest man she'd ever met, but that wasn't what riveted her attention. It was his tie—his tie which was covered with large purple elephants.

'I do want Plastic Surgery,' she replied, dragging her gaze away from his tie with difficulty. 'I'm their new SHO.'

'Oh, be still my beating heart,' he exclaimed clutching at his chest dramatically. 'You mean you and I are actually going to be working together?'

'Working together?' she repeated. 'I'm sorry, but—'

'Jack Reid,' he interrupted, clasping her hand and kissing

it. 'Bachelor of this parish, connoisseur of fine wines and beautiful women, and, in my spare time, anaesthetist to the eminent Mr Davies, esteemed boss of Plastics. If you're our new SHO, you must be—'

'Peggie O'Neill.' She laughed, extracting her hand gently. 'Spinster from County Clare, complete philistine when it comes to any kind of wine, but a girl who can recognise a flirt a mile off when she sees one.'

A broad grin lit up his face. 'Shrewd as well as pretty— the perfect combination. What say you and I go out to dinner tonight to welcome you to Lizzie's?' he continued as the elevator reached the second floor and they both got out. 'I know the perfect place—very quiet, great food, wonderful music—'

'And the address, if I'm not very much mistaken, is 21 Crown Circus,' declared a pretty girl with shining brown hair cut into a bob as she joined them. 'Tell the girl the truth, you wretch—this perfect place is your flat.'

The anaesthetist stuck out his tongue at her. 'Have a heart, Sall.'

'I do, and the only reason it's still intact is because I've never been stupid enough to go out with you,' she replied without rancour. 'Sally Cooper,' she continued, seeing Peggie's enquiring look at her black trousers and white shirt with green epaulettes. 'Staff nurse in this madhouse, and you are…?'

'Peggie O'Neill—the new SHO—but, please, call me Peggie.'

'I thought you weren't due to start until tomorrow?' the staff nurse declared.

'I'm not,' Peggie replied, 'but Mr Davies said if I came in today he could show me round the department as there weren't any clinics on a Sunday.'

'Which should only take him a couple of hours at the most,' Jack observed. 'Now, as luck would have it, I have the afternoon off—'

'Oh, give the girl a break, Jack.' Sally groaned as Peggie shook her head and chuckled. 'Haven't you got something important to do—like washing your hair, bringing your little black book up to date?'

The anaesthetist opened his eyes very wide. 'Do mine ears deceive me, or is the divine Sall trying—oh, so very subtly—to tell me my presence might be unwanted?'

'Got it in one,' she retorted, though her lips twitched.

'Your wish is my command.' He grinned. 'See you around, Peggie—and I'll take a rain check on that dinner.'

The staff nurse shook her head as he walked away. 'That man's getting worse every day.'

'But you like him,' Peggie observed shrewdly.

Sally looked as though she was about to deny it, then sighed. 'I do, which is why I have absolutely no intention of ever getting involved with him. Oh, don't get me wrong,' she continued as Peggie gazed at her questioningly. 'There's no real harm in Jack if all you're wanting is a brief fling, but there's no way I'm going out with a man who's dated practically every nurse at Lizzie's, not to mention a man who has such appalling taste in ties.'

'You mean he actually has more like that?' Peggie gasped. 'I thought it was just a one-off aberration.'

Sally shook her head and laughed, and beckoned to the plump, bespectacled, middle-aged woman who had just emerged from a door marked 'Office'.

'Marge—Marge, come and meet Dr O'Neill before she starts thinking everyone who works in Plastics is completely insane. Peggie, meet Marge MacLeod, our long-suffering receptionist.'

'Pleased to meet you, Dr O'Neill.' The receptionist smiled. 'Mr Davies isn't expecting you until eleven.'

'I know. Look, if I'm in the way—'

'Of course you're not,' the receptionist exclaimed. 'Sally, why don't you take Dr O'Neill along to the staff room and make her a cup of coffee? I'd do it myself but the boss is in an absolutely foul temper this morning.'

'So what else is new?' Sally said dryly.

'Oh, come on, be fair,' Marge protested. 'The poor man can't have had more than three hours' sleep in the last three days, and the burns case he operated on yesterday died early this morning.'

'OK, OK,' Sally said, holding up her hands in mock apology. 'So he's got an excuse today, but pardon me if I don't dash along to his room to dispense tea and sympathy.'

The receptionist tried to look severe, failed miserably, and when she disappeared back into her office, chuckling under her breath, Peggie turned to Sally quizzically.

'I gather Mr Davies isn't normally the most sweet-tempered of men?'

'You could say that. His last SHO only lasted three months.'

'Three months!' Peggie gasped.

Sally nodded. 'My advice if you want to survive around here is keep your head down, say nothing, and maybe God won't notice you.'

'God?' Peggie echoed, puzzled.

'Mr Gareth Owen Davies, our esteemed, revered and very much feared sharp-tongued consultant,' Sally replied with a mock bow. 'Otherwise known to us lesser mortals as God.'

'Does he know it?' Peggie couldn't help but laugh as they went into the staff room.

'I doubt it. Gareth doesn't engage in idle chit-chat with his staff. Come to think of it, Gareth doesn't ''chat'' to anyone full stop.'

For a moment Peggie's heart sank, but she rallied. 'I believe talented people can often be very demanding.'

'Gareth isn't demanding—he's bloody impossible.'

'But—'

'Look, I admire him hugely,' Sally continued as Peggie

gazed at her in dismay. 'He's a gifted surgeon—in fact he's probably the most gifted surgeon I've ever worked with—but when it comes to getting along with people… Frankly a rabid rat would be more popular.'

'Poor Mrs Davies,' Peggie murmured as the staff nurse rinsed two cups under the tap, then filled them with coffee.

'There isn't one. There isn't even, as far as anyone knows, an ex Mrs Davies or a girlfriend. The man's only thirty-six yet he eats, sleeps and breathes work. Hey, you might get on OK with him,' Sally continued, seeing Peggie's troubled expression. 'Jack does—though to be honest he's so thick-skinned he wouldn't recognise a snub if it bit him—but Tom's worked for Gareth for three years and survived.'

'Tom?' Peggie questioned.

'Tom Kerr—our specialist registrar. Very down-to-earth, very capable, and a lovely guy. He married Jane Darnley who used to work in Radiology, and they have a super little girl called Beth.'

'Who else works in the department?' Peggie asked with interest, accepting the coffee Sally was holding out to her.

Sally kicked off her shoes and curled up in one of the seats. 'Angel Matibele's our other staff nurse. She's really good with the kids who attend our clinics but unfortunately she's leaving in July to have a baby and God is spitting mad about that.'

'Mr Davies doesn't like women having babies, or he doesn't like babies?' Peggie declared, aghast.

'God doesn't like change, and someone leaving to have a baby means change. Frankly, I think he'd staff his department entirely with men if he could, so messy things like pregnancy couldn't upset his routine.'

'You make it sound like he doesn't like women,' Peggie murmured with a slight frown.

'I don't think he does particularly.' Sally laughed. 'We're too emotional, you see, and Gareth is logic through and through. Now, where was I?' She frowned. 'Oh, yes, there's David Chang—came into nursing late but he's a natural at it. Our student nurse, Daisy Swan—a bit nervous but her heart's in the right place. Bob Bremen, who's doing his six-month pre-reg with us—'

'Enough, enough!' Peggie protested. 'I'm never going to be able to remember the names of all these people!'

'You will.' Sally chuckled, then groaned as she glanced down at her watch. 'I'm sorry but I have to go. Tom's taking skin grafts this morning and I'm assisting. Will you be OK here on your own, or would you like me to take you over to Pharmacy to meet the gang there?'

'I think I'd rather just sit here and soak up the atmosphere, if you don't mind,' Peggie replied.

'Soak up the atmosphere?' Sally echoed, her grey eyes dancing.

Peggie chuckled. 'I know it sounds stupid, but you see I've wanted to work here ever since I started my training at the Belfast General, and now, to be actually here...'

The staff nurse shook her head. 'I'll remind you of that in a couple of weeks' time when you're tearing your hair out and telling me you want to leave!'

'I won't ever do that.' Peggie laughed.

And she wouldn't, she thought as Sally disappeared out the door. Getting this job had been a dream come true, and she didn't care if Gareth Davies was the original bear with a sore head to work for. Just to be able to watch him operate, to maybe learn some of his skills— It would be worth any amount of grouchiness.

The one thing she'd better not be, however, was late for her appointment with him, but she had plenty of time yet as a quick glance at the staff room clock confirmed. Plenty of time to take her empty cup over to the sink and sigh ruefully at the reflection which gazed back at her from the mirror above it.

Why couldn't she have inherited her father's height and

slim build—or, better yet, her mother's stunning auburn hair and beautiful blue eyes? OK, so her shoulder-length hair was thick and black and wavy, but that didn't make up for being five feet nothing, with a pair of boring brown eyes, a snub nose, and a figure which was most definitely rounded.

She sighed, then suddenly whirled round to look at the staff room clock again. Surely it had said half-past ten when Sally had made the coffee, and that must have been at least half an hour ago?

A quick glance at her watch confirmed it. It was a minute to eleven. The clock had stopped.

She could still make it, she thought as she flew out of the staff room. OK, she might arrive a bit dishevelled and breathless, but she could still be on time if she ran as fast as she could.

And she did run as fast as she could, down the corridor, round the corner, and straight into a tall figure, sending the bundle of files he was carrying scattering everywhere and herself tumbling to the floor.

'Oh, I'm so sorry,' she gasped, totally winded. 'I—'

'*You* again!'

She might well have said the same, she thought as she gazed up into a pair of familiar green eyes, if she hadn't caught sight of the name tag on his pristine striped shirt. Make me wrong, she prayed, squeezing her eyes tight shut in the hope that when she opened them again it would all be a mistake, but it wasn't.

Awkwardly she got to her feet, and even more awkwardly she held out her hand. 'Mr...Mr Davies...I'm Peggie O'Neill.'

'And I'm sure when they carry me off to A and E with a broken arm or a broken leg it will please me no end to know that,' he began, 'but I fail to see...' He paused, the frown lines on his forehead deepened, then he gazed heavenwards in disbelief. 'Oh, please God, tell me I'm wrong. Don't tell me you're my new SHO!'

'I'm afraid I am, sir,' she replied with an attempt at a smile. 'I can only apologise—'

'*Apologise?*' he repeated, his expression furious. 'Do you have *any* idea how many files are down there? It will take me hours—if not days—to get them back into order!'

'No, it won't,' she declared, hurriedly picking up some of the papers nearest to her. 'Every sheet has the patient's name on it, and if I collect all the ones with the same name—'

'Don't touch them!' he roared. 'Don't lay a finger on them, OK?'

'But—'

'What the hell were you doing careering down the corridor in the first place?' he demanded, getting down on his hands and knees and beginning to gather up the scattered files. 'Is the hospital on fire—has some escaped psychopath broken into the building?'

'I thought I was going to be late for my appointment with you,' she replied miserably, noticing quite illogically that now his hair was dry it was black with tiny threads of silver at the temples. 'I know how valuable your time is—'

'Not on this evidence, you don't,' he interrupted crisply.

She crimsoned and got down on her knees beside him. 'Please—won't you at least let me try to help you? If the two of us tackle it—'

'Whoa, novel approach there, Gareth.' Jack grinned as he appeared round the corner. 'Get the girl on her knees and it's harder for her to escape!'

'Something you want, Jack?' he demanded, glaring up at him. 'Because if there isn't…'

'Six-year-old on her way up to theatre from A and E,' the anaesthetist declared, instantly professional.

'Condition?' Gareth asked, rising to his feet, the files forgotten.

'According to A and E three fractured ribs, and extensive tissue damage to her face.'

'Sally—'

'Already in theatre, and Tom says he can assist if you want.'

Quickly Gareth began to follow the anaesthetist down the corridor, only to swing round suddenly and stare at Peggie. 'Tell Tom I won't need him,' he murmured. 'Dr O'Neill will assist.'

The papers Peggie had been collecting slipped from her fingers. 'M-me?'

His lip curled. 'I don't see anyone else around here with that surname, but if you don't feel up to it...?'

Her chin came up at that. 'I'm your SHO, Mr Davies. Of course I'm up to it.'

'He does it to everyone,' Sally said reassuringly some time later when Peggie had finished scrubbing up and was standing nervously in the middle of the changing room, heartily wishing she'd never been born. 'Deliberately throws you in at the deep end to see if you'll sink or swim. My first case was a three-year-old with ninety per cent burns and I threw up in the toilets for hours afterwards.'

'I can understand his reasoning but does he have to be so—?'

'Ready, Dr O'Neill?' Gareth exclaimed, banging open the door of the changing room without warning.

As I'll ever be, she wanted to reply, but she simply nodded and followed him through to the theatre.

'Status, Jack?' he asked, glancing over to the anaesthetist who was already in position.

'Sleeping like a baby. Heart-rate a little fast, but not worryingly so, pulse 110 over 60, breathing fine.'

'Thank God she didn't go through the windscreen,' Gareth observed, gazing critically at the little girl who was fast asleep on the operating table. 'With luck we should be able to get reasonably good results from accurate tissue replacement and vertical sutures.'

Unconsciously Peggie nodded. Vertical sutures gave the best cosmetic results in a child this young, but if Tracy Ward had gone through the windscreen she would have suffered shelving lacerations, and, no matter how good a surgeon Gareth was, there was no way he could have sutured vertically without cutting away too much viable tissue. The little girl would have been scarred for life.

'OK, Dr O'Neill,' Gareth declared, breaking suddenly into her thoughts. 'What's the first step in plastics when dealing with a facial injury?'

'A-assess the damage and decide whether simple suturing or skin grafts will be required,' she replied, considerably flustered.

'Wrong,' he replied curtly. 'The first step is make sure all the dirt has been removed from the wounds. If you don't your unfortunate patient will end up with tattooed scarring which is virtually impossible to remove once the wound has healed.'

Peggie flushed under her mask as Sally shot her a sympathetic glance. She knew perfectly well that removal of dirt was the first priority in plastic surgery. Why, oh, why, had she given him the wrong answer?

Because he's intimidating you, she realised. Because in the theatre, dressed in his blue scrubs, he seems so much bigger, so much more awesome. OK, she'd already known he was a big man—in fact, after cannoning into him twice in one day she was going to have the bruises tomorrow to prove it—but standing next to him she knew exactly why his staff referred to him as God. The man exuded authority and ability.

'Always ensure the liquid you use to clean and sterilise the patient's skin won't stain,' he continued as he began cleaning the dirt from Tracy's face. 'Cetrimide and an aqueous solution of Hibitane are good. The last thing you want is to use something which will obscure the skin colour, particularly if you're planning on taking skin grafts for the face.'

She nodded, but when she stepped back slightly to let Sally get nearer to the operating table with her trolley of instruments his head came up immediately.

'You're not going to be much use to me at the back of the theatre, Doctor.'

'I was trying not to get in the way,' she protested, stung by the sarcasm in his voice.

'That must be a first,' he observed and she flushed even more.

'Mr Davies—'

'What's the secret of good cosmetic results?' he interrupted.

For a second Peggie hesitated, then took a deep breath. 'Cutting conservatively. Only ever remove obviously non-viable tissue because what you're aiming for is to replace as much of the skin into its normal position as possible.'

'And how would you know whether a piece of traumatised tissue is viable and should be conserved, or whether it should be excised?' he demanded.

'Circulation?' she hazarded, praying she was right, and to her relief saw a glimmer of approval in his green eyes.

'Circulation.' He nodded. 'If the skin blanches when pressure is exerted and then returns to its original colour that's a good sign—as is the presence of bleeding from the cut edge of the tissue. Vital signs, Jack?' he continued, glancing over to him.

'Fine, Gareth. No problems at all,' the anaesthetist answered, and waited only until the surgeon's back was turned before winking encouragingly across at Peggie.

A bubble of amusement welled in her and she crushed it down quickly. It was like being in an exam, she thought ruefully—an exam conducted by the toughest adjudicator in the world—but at least Jack and Sally seemed to be on her side.

'Any good at jigsaws, Dr O'Neill?'

'S-sorry?' she faltered, turning quickly back to Gareth.

'Jigsaws—do you like doing jigsaws?'

'I do, but—'

'Much of plastic surgery is not unlike starting a jigsaw— a jigsaw in which some of the pieces are often missing. If you can get two pieces of skin which definitely fit sutured together, fresh parts of the jigsaw will more easily fall into place. Never forget, Dr O'Neill, that time spent accurately fitting a jigsaw of tissue is never wasted. Bonney's Blue, Sally.'

The staff nurse handed him the mixture of gentian violet, brilliant green, alcohol and water and Peggie watched with interest as he gently tattooed the mixture onto Tracy's lower cheek before making his incision to remove the damaged tissue.

'You're using Bonney's Blue because your incision is going to be curved, aren't you?' she observed without thinking. 'I mean, with the incision being curved there's bound to be a certain amount of distortion when you start suturing,' she added hurriedly as his eyebrows rose. 'And it's easier to match the two folds of skin if you tattoo matching points first.'

'Perfectly correct,' he answered with what to her sounded like grudging approval. 'So what type of suture would you use?'

'Interrupted ones would give the best cosmetic results.'

'Choice of suture material?'

'Nylon or prolene,' she replied, secure in the knowledge she was on safer ground here. 'Surgeons used to use silk but it's considered very old-fashioned now.'

'I'm afraid you'll have to consider me old-fashioned,' Gareth declared dryly. 'Nylon or prolene are all very well in their way but to achieve the correct tension when tying a suture, to make sure the wound edges are accurately opposed, nothing—to my mind—betters silk.'

'But don't you find skin reacts badly to silk?' she observed, refusing to back down.

'Only until the suture is removed, and, until you can offer me documented proof that the results achieved with synthetics are any better than those achieved with silk, I will continue to be old-fashioned. Forceps, Sally.'

Peggie bit her lip as Sally handed them to him.

Why, oh, why, had she presumed to argue with him? He was the expert, not her, and he was good, she thought, as she watched him beginning to suture the wounds in Tracy's face using the finest of curved needles clamped between the end of a pair of five-centimetre-long forceps. He might be as abrasive as hell, but he was good—breathtakingly so.

'OK, let's see what you can do, Dr O'Neill,' he suddenly declared. 'Finish suturing Tracy's chin for me.'

For a second she panicked, then took his place at the operating table.

This was why she'd applied for the job at Lizzie's. This was what all her years of training had been about, but it didn't take her long to discover that wanting to work with the eminent Gareth Davies, and having his steely gaze on her efforts, were two entirely different things.

'Personally I prefer toothed forceps for holding the needle,' he commented the minute she selected a pair of non-toothed ones from Sally's trolley.

Well, I don't, she wanted to reply, but said nothing.

'Don't forget to ensure the needle takes an equal bite of skin from each side,' he continued as she began to stitch. 'The last thing you want is one half of the skin inverting. You'll end up with a very bad scar if that happens.'

He was treating her like a fifth-year medical student, she thought angrily, but she wasn't a student who had just been let loose on her first patient. She might not be in his league when it came to operating skills, but she wasn't an idiot, and one day she intended to be as good as he was.

Clearly he didn't have faith in her because when she gritted her teeth and tried to ignore him he suddenly exclaimed, 'You're not rotating your wrist enough. Your hand, forceps, and needle should be part of one fluid movement so your first suture is perfect. If you have to take it out and start again, all you'll end up with is a moth-eaten wound edge.'

He was flustering her, that was the trouble, she realised, feeling a trickle of sweat run down her back. Normally she would have been able to suture the wound perfectly but it was damn near impossible to function normally when a pair of cold green eyes were surveying her so intently.

'OK, that'll do,' he said when Peggie had finally placed the last stitch under Tracy's chin and straightened up with relief. 'Dressings, Sally.'

Quickly the staff nurse applied a single layer of tulle gras to Tracy's face which would allow the passage of any discharge from the girl's wounds and also—because of its petroleum jelly base—make it easier to remove later. Then very carefully she added a layer of gauze followed by a crêpe bandage and Elastoplast to give both a cushioned pressure and to ensure Tracy's face was kept as immobile as possible until her wounds had healed.

With the child safely dispatched to Recovery under the care of Sally and Jack, Peggie followed Gareth thankfully into the changing room to find a burly, bearded man waiting for them.

'Tom Kerr—specialist registrar,' he declared, holding out his hand to her with a smile as she gazed at him questioningly. 'I thought I'd stick around in case you needed any moral support after your baptism of fire, but I doubt if you need any—does she, boss?'

Gareth threw his cap into the laundry basket. 'Dr O'Neill merely inserted a few sutures—a task which any halfway decent GP could have accomplished just as easily. Only time will tell if she's got what it takes for plastic surgery.'

A surge of anger flooded through her at the injustice of his remark, but it was Tom who exclaimed, 'Oh, be fair, Gareth! The last thing the girl expected was to be pitched into surgery the minute she arrived.'

'Then she should have anticipated it,' he retorted. 'Plastics isn't a nine-to-five job.'

'I know it isn't,' Peggie said quickly, seeing real anger appear on the specialist registrar's face. 'Just as I know I have a lot to learn—'

'You have *everything* to learn, Dr O'Neill,' Gareth interrupted. 'The powers that be might have given you a fancy new title but to me you're nothing more than a newly qualified doctor who's scarcely out of med school and I suggest you don't forget it.'

Tears pricked at the backs of her eyes as he strode out of the changing room and she crushed them down resolutely. She was not going to cry. She was not going to give him the satisfaction of knowing he could make her cry, but it was a damn close thing and Tom clearly sensed it.

'Don't take it to heart, love,' he murmured awkwardly. 'He's had a rough few days—'

'No, it's more than that,' she interrupted, her throat so tight it hurt. 'I know I got off on the wrong foot with him—'

'It wouldn't have mattered which foot you got off on.' The specialist registrar sighed. 'The plain truth is Gareth didn't want a woman for this job but Martyn Lennard overruled him.'

'Why on earth should the hospital manager overrule him?' she protested. 'He doesn't know me.'

'No, but he's very politically correct, is Martyn.'

'Politically correct?'

'Think about it, love,' Tom said gently. 'Angel

Matibele's from Nigeria, David Chang's both oriental and a man, but—'

'You've no female doctor on the staff,' Peggie finished for him with dawning comprehension. 'I'm the token woman doctor—that's what you're saying, isn't it?'

'Look, the one thing Gareth respects is talent,' Tom continued as she stared at him unhappily. 'Show him you're good, and he'll come round—I know he will.'

Oh, she would show him she was good, she vowed as she walked into one of the changing cubicles and began pulling off her theatre clothes. She would show him she was good if it killed her. He was going to see she was the best damn SHO he'd ever had and then, when he turned round and praised her, she was going to spit in his stunning green eyes.

Chapter Two

IT WASN'T often Peggie lost her temper. In fact it was common knowledge to her friends and family that she invariably backed away from arguments rather than confronted them, but there were times when even she snapped, and today was one of those times.

Today she was going to talk to Mr Gareth Owen Davies. Today she was going to tell him she'd had enough of being stuck in Marge's office reading files until her eyes ached and her head felt dizzy. Today she was going to say she knew perfectly well that what he called familiarising herself with the work of the department was, in fact, his way of ensuring she kept as far away from him as possible.

'Everything OK, Peggie?' Angel Matibele asked, seeing her determined step.

'Not yet, Angel,' she answered through clenched teeth, 'but it will be.'

The staff nurse's eyebrows rose but Peggie didn't elaborate. This wasn't a subject for staff-room gossip. This was between her and Gareth Davies.

Quickly she walked down the corridor to his consulting room only to come to a disappointed halt. His door was slightly ajar and she could hear him talking to Tom Kerr. It was just typical, she thought vexedly. She'd just spent the better part of an hour psyching herself up to speak to the damn man and now she wasn't going to have the opportunity. Later, she told herself firmly, she would have it out with him later, but she had scarcely begun retracing her steps when the subject of their conversation became all too unfortunately clear.

'The girl's a walking disaster area, Tom.'

'Oh, come on, Gareth, just because you didn't want a woman for this job doesn't mean Peggie—'

'And not just a walking disaster. She looks about twelve.'

'If you think she looks twelve you need your eyes tested,' the specialist registrar retorted. 'And her appearance isn't the issue,' he continued as Gareth tried to interrupt. 'The real question is whether she's any good at her job, and keeping her stuck amongst the files sure as hell isn't the way to find out.'

'I'm the boss of this unit—'

'Yes, you are, but the one thing I never thought you were was prejudiced!'

'Tom—Tom, let's talk about this rationally—'

But the specialist registrar didn't appear to be in the mood to talk. There was the sound of a chair being pulled angrily across the floor, the unmistakable echo of footsteps, and before Peggie could move Tom had banged out of Gareth's consulting room and seen her.

'I don't need to ask if you heard all that,' he declared, a deep flush of embarrassed colour appearing on his normally genial face. 'Peggie, I don't know what's got into him—I really don't—but he'll come round—'

'When, Tom?' she protested. 'I've already been here a fortnight. Am I supposed to wait until I collect my pension before he decides I might be trusted enough to do the laundry requisitions?'

The specialist registrar looked concerned. 'You mean you're going to have it out with him?'

She drew herself up to her full five feet nothing. 'Too damned right, I am.'

A small smile curved Tom's lips. 'He'll be spitting mad, you know.'

'I don't care if he foams at the mouth,' she replied tartly.

The smile on Tom's face widened. 'Go get him, tiger—and good luck!'

She didn't need luck, she told herself as she knocked on Gareth's door. She was simply going to tell him she'd had enough, and if he didn't like it— Well, there were other plastic surgery units, other surgeons, and other SHO posts. And it didn't matter if they weren't as good as this one— at least she might get the opportunity to do what she'd been trained for.

'Something you want, Dr O'Neill?' Gareth asked, glancing up from his desk with a frown. 'I'm very busy—'

'This won't take long,' she interrupted, sitting down determinedly.

His eyebrows rose, then he put down the papers he'd been reading and surveyed her coolly. 'You have a problem?'

'Yes, I have, and it's you. Look, I know you didn't want me for this job,' she continued as his jaw dropped. 'I know you think women are too emotional and don't make good plastic surgeons—'

'Who told you that?' he demanded, sitting suddenly bolt upright in his seat.

'It's common knowledge,' she replied. 'I can't help my sex—there's nothing I can do about it—but you haven't even given me a chance. I'm good—nothing like as skilled as you are, of course, and perhaps I never will be—but I'm damned if I'm going to let you treat me like some sort of filing clerk.'

'Dr O'Neill—'

'All through my training I dreamt of working here,' she continued, knowing full well she was undoubtedly signing her own dismissal form but no longer caring. 'All through those long, difficult years the one thing that kept me going was the hope of maybe working here one day with you, and when I got this job…it was like…it was like winning the lottery.'

'Dr O'Neill—'

'Oh, I know that probably sounds really pathetic to

you—typical woman—far too emotional,' she declared, dashing a hand across her eyes where to her annoyance tears were beginning to form. 'You're the great Gareth Davies—head of your own department, master of all you survey. No wonder your staff call you God—'

'They call me what?' he exclaimed, his black eyebrows snapping down.

'God. It's because of your initials,' she explained as his frown deepened, 'and because of the skill you have, and…and because of the way you behave.'

'I see,' he said slowly. 'Peggie—'

'All I'm trying to say is, if you really don't want me here,' she continued, trying to sound calm but unfortunately her voice betrayed her, 'I'd far rather you just said so and I'll go, because, no matter what you think, this is the work I want to do, it's what I've always wanted to do, and I'm damned well going to do it!'

For a moment he said nothing. For a moment it was so quiet in his consulting room all she could hear was the unsteady thud of her own heartbeat and the rhythmic tick of the clock on his desk, then he cleared his throat. 'Are you finished?'

She straightened her back and managed to meet his gaze squarely. 'Yes, yes, I'm finished.'

'Then I want to apologise.'

This time it was her jaw that dropped. 'W-what?' she stammered faintly.

'Even God can get it wrong sometimes,' he said with a small smile, but to his dismay she didn't smile back. She simply looked stunned.

Well, she certainly couldn't be any more stunned than he felt, he decided.

All too clearly he found himself remembering how his own first consultant had treated him like dirt and how he'd vowed then that, if he ever made it, he would never treat another human being the same way. How could he have forgotten? How could he have forgotten it was only his own dreams and aspirations which had kept him going through those miserable years?

And it wasn't just her he'd treated badly, he thought with horror. She'd said his staff called him God, and he knew they didn't mean it as a compliment. They meant he was overbearing, didactic, and inflexible—all the qualities he loathed in others.

Why had nobody ever pointed it out to him—why had nobody ever told him he had become a tyrant? Because nobody else had possessed the guts, he thought wryly. Nobody but this earnest girl with her eager shining face who looked so young and vulnerable.

And that was the trouble, he realised. It wasn't that he had desperately wanted a male colleague—though after what had happened with Marianne he would certainly have preferred one. It wasn't even that she had cannoned into him twice in the same day when he'd been exhausted from lack of sleep and feeling lousy because he'd lost a patient.

It was her air of vulnerability which rattled him. It was that same air of vulnerability which had made him feel uncomfortable even before he'd known who she was. Somehow it had touched him. Somehow he'd sensed this girl could unlock a door within himself—a door he wanted kept very firmly closed—and he'd wanted to keep as far away from her as possible.

'Is there something wrong, Mr Davies?' she asked, clearly unnerved by his intent gaze.

Ye gods, she was actually blushing, he thought, watching the tide of pink creep across her cheeks with fascination. The women he'd known in the past hadn't blushed—they probably hadn't known how to since they were eight years old—and yet she did, and to his dismay he found his fingers itching to trace the path of that slow wash of colour.

Abruptly he got to his feet. 'I'm going down to IC to

take some split-skin grafts and to check on Tracy Ward. Would you like to come with me?'

'Really?' she gasped. 'You mean it?'

Boy, but he'd obviously made a wonderful impression on his staff, he thought bitterly as he nodded. Even this girl was in awe of him—the man who had once been the butt of so many jokes at university because of his second-hand clothes and thick Welsh accent.

'Of course I mean it,' he said with difficulty. 'We can walk and talk at the same time.'

He might be able to, Peggie thought as he strode out of his consulting room, but she had almost to run to keep up with him.

'You'll have noticed from our files that our patients are either brought up directly from A and E, come to us via Intensive Care after they've been stabilised, or are referred directly to us by their GPs,' he observed as he swept down the plastic surgery unit. 'In many cases it can take years for our work to show results, which is one of our major problems. Adults can at least understand the need for more surgery. To a small child all it means is more pain.'

'It must be very difficult at times, Mr Davies,' she replied.

'It can be—and, for heaven's sake, call me Gareth. Hospital is frightening enough for children without any added formality, and we are colleagues, remember, Peggie.'

'Yes—yes, of course we are,' she managed to reply as they passed Tom Kerr and she saw his stunned expression—a stunned expression which was very swiftly replaced by a broad grin and the thumbs-up sign.

If the specialist registrar was amazed by this unexpected turn of events it was as nothing to how she was feeling, she thought as Gareth led the way downstairs. She'd fully expected to be out on her ear after her outburst, and yet here she was being suddenly whisked down to see two patients, and being told she was part of the team.

Cautiously she risked a quick glance up at the man at her side. He looked the same, he certainly sounded the same, but he very clearly wasn't. Quite what had brought about this change was a mystery, and all she could do was hope it lasted.

'How's Tracy this morning?' Gareth asked as Sam Harrison, the red-haired, bespectacled consultant of Intensive Care, beamed a welcome at them.

'Good. I think we should be able to transfer her down to Surgical in a couple of days.'

'No sign of haematoma?'

The consultant shook his head. 'Sally did her job well.'

And she had, Peggie thought, remembering the care with which the staff nurse had applied Tracy's dressings. And care was vital. Complications after plastic surgery were nearly always caused by haematoma—a localised collection of clotted blood caused by bleeding from a ruptured blood vessel—and the best way to avoid it was by meticulous wound dressing.

'And Jonah Morton?' Gareth continued. 'How is he?'

Sam Harrison grimaced. 'Stable most of the time but his heart rate has a worrying tendency to shoot about all over the place. I've moved him into isolation for you.'

'Poor Jonah's in a bit of a mess,' Gareth explained as he led the way to the changing room. 'He got hold of a box of matches and has third degree burns to his face, arms, and hands to show for it.'

'How old is he?' Peggie asked.

'Just five, poor little chap.'

There was real compassion in his face—compassion that completely softened his normally harsh features, making him seem younger, kinder, and strangely—bewilderingly—attractive.

'Something wrong?' he asked as a small frown creased her forehead.

'No—nothing,' she said quickly.

For a moment she thought he might press her, but to her relief he pulled two sets of theatre scrubs out of the sterilising unit and handed one to her. 'They'll probably be far too big for you, but do the best you can.'

They were too big, but she'd had this problem before and a judicious rolling up of the trouser legs solved the problem. What it didn't solve, however, was the question of why she'd suddenly found herself thinking that Gareth Davies was actually rather an attractive man. And it certainly didn't explain the silly little jump her heart gave as she came out of the changing cubicle and found him waiting for her.

It's the clothes, she told herself as he held back the door of the changing room with his elbows and she found herself noticing that his forearms were not only remarkably muscular but also covered with fine dark hair. Some women were turned on by a man in uniform, others by the sight of a man in a black dinner jacket and bow tie. Her thing was clearly theatre scrubs.

The fact that this had never happened to her before, she chose to ignore.

'You said you were taking split-skin grafts this morning?' she declared, determinedly professional.

'In a burns case like Jonah's, split-skin grafts give maximum coverage while still leaving the sweat glands intact,' he replied as he led the way through to Isolation. 'As the burns we'll be covering initially are on his arms, a perfect colour match isn't so important. Oh, and in case you're too embarrassed to ask when you see him,' he added, 'colour match is every bit as tricky on a black skin as it is on a white.'

She didn't need him to tell her that. One of the first burns cases she'd helped treat when she'd been training had been a child from Zambia and she'd been amazed at the number of different shades of black there were.

'Cheer up, Jonah,' Gareth exclaimed as they entered the

isolation unit and found Sister Gilbert standing beside an obviously very scared little boy lying on a trolley. 'I promised you wouldn't feel a thing even though you're wide awake, and I never break a promise.'

'Did you manage to keep your other promise?' the little boy whispered.

For an answer Gareth dived into the pocket of his theatre pyjamas and produced a photograph. 'One fully autographed picture of the members of Arsenal football team as promised.'

Jonah's eyes lit up with delight and Gareth turned to Sister Gilbert.

'Did you remember to add hyaluronidase to the solution when you injected the local anaesthetic, Sister?'

A wry smile curved her lips. 'When did I ever forget, Mr Davies?'

To Peggie's surprise he actually coloured but, if she was surprised by the sight of a clearly deeply embarrassed Gareth Davies, Sister Gilbert was obviously thunderstruck when he muttered, 'My apologies, Sister.'

Wonders would never cease, Peggie decided, biting down hard on her lip to suppress her laughter at the sight of Sister Gilbert's bemused expression as she gently eased Jonah's leg round so the inside of his thigh was pointing upwards, ready for Gareth to take his first graft. It really was a new, improved Gareth Davies this morning, and she, for one, fully intended to enjoy the phenomenon.

One thing about him couldn't possibly be improved, however, and that was his skill. Keeping the Humby—the combined small roller and blade which he was using to take the grafts—moving in unison with the board he pressed down onto Jonah's skin to keep it steady was hard enough, but he never once used the Humby's gauge to check for the thickness of the graft he was taking. He simply held it up to the light to check the clearance between the blade and the roller.

'It comes with practice,' he observed, catching her gaze on him. 'What you want is a clearance of a little less than 0.5mm for a graft of average thickness but you'll soon find your hand and eye are the best judge.'

They might be for him, she thought enviously, but she could never envisage herself ever being that confident.

'Try it,' he declared, as though reading her mind.

'Are you sure?' she gasped.

'I wouldn't have said so otherwise,' he replied briskly. 'And Jonah doesn't mind, do you, Jonah?'

The little boy looked highly dubious and Peggie smiled down at him. 'If I hurt you, may my fingernails turn green and my hair fall out.'

Jonah giggled and visibly relaxed.

'You want the blade to move smoothly to and fro over the skin when you're cutting, but the skin not to move at all,' Gareth observed as Peggie took his place beside the trolley and Sister Gilbert turned Jonah over onto his stomach so that Peggie could reach the back of his thigh. 'If you keep the skin and the surface of the blade well lubricated with liquid paraffin that should reduce any drag.'

She nodded but as she began cutting he soon realised she really didn't need his advice.

She was good. She had instinctive hands and a real feeling for skin, which was rare. With the right training she could be exceptional—though at the moment, judging by the frown on her face, she obviously didn't think so.

'You make it look so easy.' She sighed as she manipulated the Humby over the back of Jonah's thigh. 'I seem to be all fingers and thumbs.'

'It needs practice,' he said encouragingly, 'and you're doing very well, believe me.'

She looked up at him quickly, a wide smile of delight on her face, and his breath caught in his throat. He'd told Tom she looked about twelve but the way his body had just reacted to that smile would have got him arrested if she'd actually been twelve.

If she'd been a particularly pretty girl he could have understood it, but she wasn't. Yes, she had rather nice thick black hair, but if you were going to be critical—and he fully intended to be critical—her nose was too small, her mouth was too wide, and she possessed a pair of very ordinary brown eyes.

No, not ordinary, he decided, unconsciously shaking his head. Her eyes laughed. When she was pleased by something, or amused, her eyes actually laughed.

'Am I doing something wrong?' she faltered, clearly misinterpreting the shake of his head.

'Not at all,' he murmured gruffly. 'As I said you're doing well—really well.'

'But not good enough.' She sighed. 'I couldn't possibly judge the thickness of a graft by eye as you do.'

'You will,' he said, pulling himself together with an effort. 'Look, it might help if you remember that a very thin graft is translucent and not unlike tissue paper,' he continued as she gazed at him, obviously unconvinced. 'A full thickness split-skin graft, on the other hand, has the colour and appearance of cadaver skin.'

'And a medium thickness split-skin graft?'

'Moderately translucent. The pattern of bleeding of the donor site can also give you an indication of thickness. The thin graft produces a high density of tiny bleeding points; the thicker graft gives a lower density of bleeding points.'

'You make it sound so simple,' she said ruefully.

'I don't intend to,' he insisted. 'Believe me, I felt totally inadequate when I first started.'

She smiled again, and this time he actually found himself smiling back.

Get a grip, Gareth, he told himself severely, seeing Sister Gilbert's astonished gaze. You're behaving like a teenager in the throws of your first crush and after Marianne and Julia you should know better—a hell of a lot better.

'I think that's enough for today, Sister,' he said, turning from the trolley abruptly. 'Jonah's getting tired, and the anaesthetic will be wearing off soon.'

It didn't take Sister Gilbert long to apply Kaltostat dressings to Jonah's donor sites, and, after telling her which painkillers he wanted the child to have when the anaesthetic had worn off, Gareth went back into the IC ward to check on Tracy Ward's sutures. Not surprisingly Sam Harrison's assessment of her condition was correct, and after signing the necessary release papers which would allow her to be transferred to the surgical ward Gareth was soon leading the way back upstairs.

'When will you be taking the full thickness skin grafts Jonah needs for his face and hands?' Peggie asked.

'In a week—ten days, tops,' Gareth replied. 'I can't afford to wait much longer—there's too much danger of a Streptococcus infection—but the problem with taking full thickness grafts is the limited number of donor sites available for a good colour match.'

'The skin on the back of the ears and on the head is good for replacing eyelid skin, isn't it?' she observed.

'It is, but though you don't get very much skin,' he replied, holding open the door of the plastic surgery unit for her. 'And though full thickness grafts most closely resemble normal skin because they consist of both epidermis and dermis, they have to be cut with a scalpel, which means if the donor area is large we're going to have to cover that with a split-skin graft.'

'What about using skin from the base of his neck or groin?' she asked, ducking under his arm and accidentally affording him a tantalising glimpse down the open V of her blouse of an expanse of smooth soft skin and a white lacy bra.

Quickly he averted his gaze. How long had it been since

he'd made love to a woman? Too long, it appeared, if the rampant reaction of his body to the glimpse of a girl's bra was anything to go by.

'The skin at the neck and groin is certainly thinner than average,' he said quickly, suddenly realising she was waiting for an answer, 'so you'd get a reasonably good colour and texture match, but again you're limited in the amount you can get unless another graft is used to cover the donor site.'

'And you can only use skin from the thigh or abdomen for his face if you're really desperate,' she said thoughtfully. 'The texture and colour match would be very poor, and as the skin is thicker the grafted area would end up looking like a mask.'

He'd been right—she was good. It would be a pleasure to teach her all he knew, and if that meant spending rather more time in her company than he suspected might be strictly comfortable... Well, it was a bridge he would cross when he reached it.

'I think it's time we started justifying your salary,' he heard himself say. 'Come along to my consulting room and I'll select some patients for you to see by yourself tomorrow.'

'You mean it?' She beamed. 'Oh, I won't let you down—I promise I won't!'

He didn't believe for one moment that she would. What concerned him more as he felt his treacherous body responding to her smile again was the realisation that he'd already reached his bridge—had in fact put one foot on it already—but there was no going back now.

Suffering, he reminded himself as he led the way along the corridor and into his consulting room, was supposed to be good for the soul. He could only hope it was good for the body too.

'This is an interesting case,' he declared, lifting the top file from the pile on his desk and handing it to her. 'Kate

Turner. Six years old, and as you can see from the photographs she has a very prominent port-wine stain on her left cheek. Unlike the stork or strawberry type of haemangioma which are very common in new-born babies, and which normally disappear by the time a child is eight or nine, Kate's haemangioma isn't going to go away unless we do something about it.'

'Surgical removal used to be the only treatment before the arrival of lasers, didn't it?' said Peggie, gazing down at the photographs he had given her.

He nodded. 'And it left the skin so badly scarred it was scarcely an improvement on the original disfigurement.'

'What kind of laser were you planning on using?' she asked, putting the photographs down. 'Argon or tuneable dye?'

'Which type would you use?' A warm smile crept over his face as she gazed at him uncertainly. 'It's not a test, Peggie. I'm just interested in hearing your opinion, that's all.'

Right now she didn't have an opinion. Right now all she was wondering was how it was possible for a particular smile to so completely change a man. And it was a very particular smile. It began at his lips, spread gradually to his eyes, and she felt her heart give that odd little flip again.

So much for it being his theatre clothes. He wasn't wearing them now, but a very ordinary—albeit clearly very expensive—green shirt and black trousers. Peanut butter, she told herself firmly. That was the last time she was ever going to have peanut butter for breakfast if it led to heart palpitations like this.

'I—um—the tuneable dye laser penetrates deeper into the dermis so the risk of any scarring after using it is very low,' she began hurriedly, making a mental note to buy marmalade before she went home tonight. 'But in expert hands the argon laser actually produces better results with dark port-wine stains.'

'So…?' he pressed.

'Not having seen the child, but judging by the apparent paleness of the lesions in these photographs, I'd opt for the tuneable dye.'

'So would I.' Quickly he riffled through his files and extracted two more. 'Billy Oswald, referred to us by his GP for possible otoplasty because of badly protruding ears, and Robbie Taylor, referred for a rhinoplasty after his nose had an unfortunate encounter with a cricket bat.'

'I'm surprised their GPs referred either of them,' she murmured, glancing through the notes. 'With the budget cutbacks nowadays, I wouldn't have been surprised if they'd considered it an unwarranted drain on their resources—vanity, if you like.'

Gareth's eyebrows suddenly snapped down. 'There is no such thing as vanity where a child is concerned. If they're being made unhappy and miserable because of their appearance, they deserve all the help they can get.'

'I didn't mean Billy and Robbie shouldn't have their operations,' she said quickly. 'What I meant was they both clearly have very understanding doctors.'

'And why the hell shouldn't they have?' he demanded. 'Everybody—*everybody*—has the right to have their personal fears and worries taken seriously!'

There was real anger in his face—an anger she could almost have sworn came of personal experience, yet there were no tell-tale marks of surgery on his face, no scars to suggest he'd undergone treatment to remove some disfigurement.

'Mr Davies—Gareth—'

He forced a smile to his lips. 'Sorry. GP funding is one of my pet crusades. I'll get off my soapbox now.'

It was more than that, she decided with a frown as he turned back to the pile of files and extracted some more. Somehow she had managed to touch a very raw nerve and she wished she knew what it was.

'It's almost time for your afternoon clinic, Gareth,' Sally declared, opening the consulting-room door.

He nodded and held out a bundle of files to Peggie. 'Take these with you. Give them a quick read through, and if there's anything you're not sure of—anything you find worrying—come and see me later.'

She took the files and had almost made her way to the door when he cleared his throat.

'Those skin grafts we took from Jonah Morton this morning. Would you like to assist me when I apply them?'

'Would I ever,' she replied, her brown eyes sparkling with pleasure.

'It will be good experience for you,' he observed, 'and the Belfast General certainly trained you well.'

'Buying your book—*The Fundamental Principles of Plastic Surgery*—helped a lot too.' She smiled.

'You bought it?' he said in surprise.

'I had to live on beans on toast for a month—' she laughed '—but it was worth every penny.'

To her surprise he frowned. 'Well, in future don't go wasting your money buying medical books. I've dozens I could lend you.'

'But I couldn't possibly—'

'End of discussion,' he said firmly. 'Anything you need in the way of medical books, just ask.'

Overwhelmed by his offer, she managed only to stammer out a disjointed thanks, but as soon as she and Sally were out in the corridor the staff nurse turned to her, her grey eyes dancing.

'I think you might have scored there.'

'Scored?' Peggie repeated, bewildered.

'I have to say "I've dozens of medical books I could lend you", isn't exactly the world's best chat-up line, but it's certainly a lot more original than Jack's restaurant ploy.'

'He wasn't chatting me up,' Peggie replied, considerably flustered. 'He was just being kind.'

'God—kind?' Sally protested. 'God's never been known to be kind to anyone, and The Siren's certainly tried hard enough to get him to notice her.'

'The Siren?'

'Frances Harper, physiotherapist linked with Plastics, twenty-seven-years old, divorced, and quite sickeningly gorgeous.'

A frown appeared on Peggie's forehead. 'I don't think I've met her.'

'Oh, you'd remember if you'd met Frances,' Sally said with feeling. 'You wouldn't believe the number of times she's dropped by the department clutching theatre tickets or dinner dance invitations.'

'She's keen on Gareth?' Peggie said slowly.

'Keen? Her tongue practically hits the carpet every time she sees him, and you can almost hear the cash register whirring in her brain.'

'The cash register…?'

'Peggie, there are women who go into the medical profession to help others, and there are those who go into it to snare a rich consultant.'

'And Frances is one of the latter?' Peggie observed, her frown deepening.

'You bet.' Sally nodded. 'She's done everything bar strip off to get him interested and it hasn't worked. Now, you—you just have to imply you can't afford to buy all the medical books you need, and bingo—he's hooked.'

'Don't be silly,' Peggie protested. 'The man's my boss…he's…he's…'

'Quite attractive if you go for the dark, brooding type.'

'He isn't—I mean, he is, but—'

'Why, Dr O'Neill, I do believe you're blushing,' Sally exclaimed with a wide grin. 'Don't tell me you're falling for the guy?'

'Of course I'm not,' Peggie retorted. 'I admire his talent, his skill, his...his...'

'Broad shoulders and cute butt?'

'Stop it, Sally,' she said sharply. 'I don't find it funny, and I don't think Mr Davies would either.'

'Hey, no offence meant,' the girl replied, holding up her hands defensively. 'You admire the man's skill—fine—end of story.'

And it was the end of the story, Peggie thought as she walked angrily down the corridor. She wasn't falling for Gareth Davies—she'd never fall for Gareth Davies in a million years. OK, so she'd found herself noticing how very muscular his forearms were, and that if he smiled a very particular smile his face was totally transformed, but that didn't mean anything.

All it meant, she told herself very firmly as she walked into her consulting room and banged the door shut, was that she was observant, which was exactly what all good surgeons were supposed to be.

Chapter Three

'VITAL signs, Jack?'

'A OK, boss.'

'Lab results, Sally?'

'No sign of any bacteria that would prevent the grafts from taking, Gareth.'

'OK, people, let's get to work,' he declared as the staff nurse opened the sterile container where Jonah Morton's grafts had been kept wrapped in saline-moistened gauze and stored at four degrees centigrade for the past ten days.

Quickly Peggie rolled out a fine sheet of aluminium foil, then paused. 'I was taught to make a pattern of the badly damaged skin before I removed it,' she said uncertainly. 'Would you rather I did it afterwards?'

'Before—after—whichever you're personally happier with,' Gareth replied. 'The most important thing is never to stretch the graft to make it fit. It will only revert to its original size.'

'Rather like trying to make a small piece of pastry fit a large pie dish,' she observed. 'It always collapses.'

'Never having made a pie, I'll take your word for it,' he declared, and she knew he was smiling at her behind his mask.

He did have nice eyes when he smiled, she decided. Deep and green and vibrant like the waters of Ballyeighter Lough back home in Ireland. And she really liked his aftershave. It wasn't sweet or cloying like the ones some men wore, but warm and comforting.

Maybe it wasn't aftershave, she thought, unable to resist taking another surreptitious sniff as he reached for his scalpel. Maybe it was just soap. Whatever it was, she had the strangest feeling she'd never forget it.

'Something the matter, Peggie?' he asked, glancing across at her with a slightly puzzled frown.

Quickly she shook her head, grateful that her surgical mask was hiding the deep blush she could feel creeping across her face. What in the world had got into her? She should be concentrating on what they were doing, not spending her time admiring a man's eyes and debating whether he was wearing aftershave or not.

'The donor sites are healing very well,' she forced herself to say as he made his first incision.

'Most do within three to four days. You get the odd awkward one, but that's generally most unusual. Could you take the sucker out, please.'

Quickly she did as he asked.

'Only ever keep the sucker in place while you're cutting,' he continued. 'The minute you've cut the skin you want, take the sucker out otherwise the bleeding will continue and you'll have the devil's own job getting the graft to "take".'

'In the Belfast General we were taught to flush out under the graft with saline once it was sutured to make sure the bed was completely dry,' Peggie observed, watching him.

'It's not a bad habit to get into,' he commented, 'but the best way to make sure of a dry field is to take your time. Always plan your operation to give the area to be grafted the longest possible time for normal haemostatic processes to become effective.'

She nodded and held out the first graft to him.

'Well done,' he said, glancing down approvingly at it. 'Many newcomers to plastics make the mistake of cutting a split-skin graft exactly to size, but you've cut it large enough not only to cover the defect but also to leave an overlap.'

'You said in your book to do that,' she confessed. 'To

always make the graft slightly larger than you need, and trim it to fit after you've sutured it in place.'

'Maybe I should ask my publishers for higher royalties if it teaches the subject so well.' He laughed.

'Maybe you should,' she agreed, laughing too.

'Patient's BP steady, pulse rate near to normal, heart rate OK—in case anyone's interested,' Jack Reid said with a grin, his eyes darting from Peggie to Gareth, then back again.

'I don't recall asking for an update, Jack, but thanks for sharing that with us,' Gareth exclaimed, his tone suddenly distinctly cool, but the anaesthetist didn't look one bit perturbed.

In fact his grin widened considerably, and Peggie noticed Sally was smiling too in a particularly annoying and knowing fashion.

The two of them were acting like a couple of overgrown teenagers, she thought vexedly, and it wasn't funny. Just because she and Gareth had shared a joke didn't mean anything. Good grief, she and old Mr Goode who ran the post office down in the shopping mall often shared a joke, and nobody made anything out of that.

'Don't cut all your sutures short when you've stitched the graft into place,' Gareth advised, clearly totally oblivious to the amused glances Sally and Jack were giving him. 'Leave some of them long. And if you find one of the skin edges dipping slightly, tie the suture knot to that side and it should level it up.'

Determinedly Peggie ignored Sally and Jack's winks and nods, and as she and Gareth painstakingly began to apply the other grafts she eventually forgot all about them in the sheer fascination of the work they were doing.

'Good work,' Gareth declared, gazing critically at her sutures once they'd finished. 'The important thing now is to apply uniform pressure to keep the grafts from moving.

To achieve that we first apply thin layers of tulle gras, then a layer of flavine wool.'

'That's why you wanted some of the sutures left long,' Peggie exclaimed as Sally carefully laid the dressings in place. 'You're going to use them to anchor the graft, wool and tulle in a single mass?'

Gareth nodded. 'More cotton wool on top helps to further diffuse the pressure, and crêpe bandages and Elastoplast complete the job. What we want is to keep the whole area immobile as well as under pressure. Immobility aids healing, and pressure prevents haematoma which might otherwise separate the graft from the bed.'

If ever she'd had any doubts about whether this was really the career she wanted, they had completely gone now as she helped him anchor the dressings in place. The work was so stimulating, so challenging, and something of her enthusiasm must have communicated itself to Gareth because as soon as they were back in the changing room he turned to her with a smile.

'You really enjoyed that, didn't you?'

'Was it so obvious?' she declared, then chuckled as his smile widened. 'I'm sorry—I guess it must all seem pretty routine to you now.'

He shook his head. 'It's never that. Each case is different—each patient brings a new challenge—and because plastic surgery techniques are changing all the time, there's always something new to learn. And talking of new things to learn—you've got Charlotte Heath coming into your clinic this afternoon, haven't you?'

'Six years old, left with residual scarring on her face after an RTA two years ago?'

He nodded. 'Would you mind if I sat in with you? I'm not questioning your ability,' he continued as a small frown creased her forehead, 'but I noticed from her file that she was treated at a hospital I've had dealings with before, and I'd like to see what the problem is.'

'I thought surgeons never criticised one another's operations.' She smiled but he, she noticed, didn't.

'This surgeon does if he sees examples of gross incompetence,' he declared, his face suddenly grim. 'Look, if you're not happy at the idea of me sitting in—'

'Of course I don't mind,' she interrupted. 'Her appointment's at four.'

'I'll see you then,' he replied, making for the changing-room door. 'And now go and get yourself some lunch—you've earned it.'

She might well have earned it, she thought, as her stomach rumbled its agreement, but lunch today would be the same as it had been for the past few weeks—one apple bought from Dunwoodys, the flower and fruit shop downstairs.

Thank God she got paid next week, she thought as she changed out of her theatre clothes and into her sweater and skirt. A diet made up largely of apples and sandwiches was beginning to make her feel distinctly light-headed, but everything in London had turned out to be so much more expensive than she'd budgeted for and there was only one way to economise.

A wry smile curved her lips as she left the hospital and made her way to Regent's Park. If there was any justice in the world she would at least have lost some weight after all this enforced starvation, but it looked as if she was destined to be one of life's chubbies.

'Lovely day, isn't it, dear?' observed the elderly gentleman who always walked his equally aged cocker spaniel in the park every morning as she sat down on her usual bench.

She smiled back. It was a lovely day. The sun was shining, the trees were green, and the daffodils were out. Spring was here and if she ignored the park signs and railings she could almost believe she was back home again on her parents' farm. And if she closed her eyes and tried really,

really hard she could almost imagine she heard the faint
bleat of new-born lambs.

'I thought I told you to have some lunch.'

Her eyes snapped open in dismay to see Gareth frowning
down at her and quickly she pushed her apple core into her
duffle-coat pocket.

'I—I've just had it,' she stammered.

'That was lunch?' he exclaimed, his frown deepening.

'I wasn't very hungry,' she mumbled, cursing her bad
luck that he should choose to go for a walk in the park
today. 'And you can't have had any lunch at all,' she
pointed out as he opened his mouth, clearly intending to
argue.

'I don't eat lunch,' he declared, sitting down beside her.
'I prefer to have a good breakfast and dinner.'

Lovingly prepared by some cordon bleu housekeeper, no
doubt, she thought enviously. She wondered where he
lived—probably in one of the exclusive executive flats near
the park, or maybe in one of those huge houses in
Kensington. Wherever it was, it was bound to be a lot more
comfortable than where she stayed.

No, that wasn't fair, she told herself. The modern block
of flatlets rented out to Lizzie's staff was a lot more attractive than any other hospital accommodation she'd ever
stayed in. It simply wasn't home.

'You must be finding it lonely living in London—knowing so few people, I mean,' he said as though reading her
mind.

'It's not too bad,' she replied, determinedly cheerful.
'My work takes up a lot of my time. And when I'm not
working, I'm studying.'

He thought it sounded a singularly empty life, but could
he honestly say his own was much better? He'd once
thought his life was fulfilling, satisfying. He'd once told
himself his work was all he needed, and yet now... Now,

he wasn't at all sure that it was, and it troubled him greatly to find himself thinking that way.

'What part of Ireland are you from?' he forced himself to ask, though in truth he suspected that, the fewer personal details he knew about the girl sitting next to him, the better it would be for his own peace of mind.

'I doubt if you've heard of it.' She smiled. 'My parents have a farm near a small village called Leoanen in County Clare.'

'And you miss it and them a lot,' he observed, leaning back against the bench to gaze at her.

She sighed. 'More than I ever thought possible.'

'And do you also miss some tall, dark, handsome Irishman?' he said before he could stop himself.

She chuckled and shook her head. 'Not a one. My sister, Sinead, says I'm too choosy.'

'It's not a bad thing to be,' he observed, annoyed with himself for having asked, and even more annoyed by the relief he felt at her answer.

'That's what I told her.' She nodded. 'My brother Patrick used to tease me all the time until Connor told him to stop, and even my sister Mary said it was getting on her nerves—'

'Patrick, Connor, Mary, Sinead?' He counted the names off his fingers with some amusement. 'How many brothers and sisters do you have?'

'That's them all.' She laughed. 'Do you have any brothers and sisters?'

'Only one sister. She lives with her husband in a village called Cefndeuddwr in North Wales, not very far from where my parents used to have their farm.'

'You're from a farming family too?' she said in surprise. 'Then you'll understand what I mean about missing it.'

His face darkened slightly. 'If there's one place I don't miss, it's my parents' farm.'

'But people are so much more friendly in the country

than they are in town, don't you think?' she pressed. 'You can never be lonely—people are always popping in for a chat.'

'People didn't often "pop" into our house,' he replied, his voice oddly clipped. 'And they "popped" in even less after my father died.'

'But—'

'I think we'd better start making our way back to the hospital,' he said, getting to his feet. 'It might be April but there's not much warmth in that sun yet.'

He was right, there wasn't, but she had the strangest feeling he had merely used the weather as an excuse to put an end to a conversation he didn't want to have and his next words confirmed it.

'How are you getting on with Sally, Angel and the rest?'

She would like to have known more about his parents' farm, and his mother and sister, but something about his expression told her the subject was very firmly closed.

'Very well, thank you,' she replied, falling into step beside him.

'They're a good crowd.' He nodded. 'Even Jack, for all his antics, is actually an excellent anaesthetist.'

'Not to mention being very fast on his feet.' She smiled.

'Fast on his feet?' he queried, glancing down at her.

She chuckled. 'He asked me out to dinner sixty seconds after we'd met.'

The words And did you go? sprang to his lips and he crushed them down resolutely. It was none of his business if Peggie had gone out with Jack—was still going out with Jack. Accepting that fact, however, didn't mean he had to like it, and he discovered he didn't.

'Jack…he has quite a reputation around the hospital,' he murmured.

'He does, doesn't he?' She laughed.

Well, if Jack was her type, so be it, he decided grimly. He'd have thought a girl like her could have done better—

a lot better—but maybe the dark shadows she'd started to acquire around her eyes weren't due to working too hard as he had thought. Maybe they were due to too many nights out—or, even worse, nights in—with Jack.

A surge of quite irrational anger flooded through him and unconsciously he quickened his stride.

'Hey, slow down,' Peggie protested. 'I've only got little legs.'

Little, but with beautifully slender calves and equally slender ankles, he found himself thinking to his great annoyance.

'I've a meeting at two o'clock with the parents of a boy who crashed through a plate-glass window,' he said brusquely. 'I don't want to be late.'

'But it's only half-past one—'

She doubted if he even heard her. He just kept on walking, and eventually she gave up the struggle to keep up with him and stared with a puzzled frown after his fast-disappearing form.

What had happened to the man who had laughed and joked with her this morning in the theatre? Even five minutes ago he had been kind enough to ask whether she was finding it lonely in London, and now he'd just walked away from her as if she didn't exist.

Desperately she racked her brains to see what she could have said that might have angered him, and eventually gave up. She had enough to cope with at the moment without spending her time trying to figure out the inner workings of Gareth Davies' mind.

'You're back early from lunch,' Sally said in surprise as Peggie came into the staff room.

'Not intentionally, believe me,' Peggie replied wryly, slipping off her duffle-coat and hanging it up. 'Any sign of any of my patients yet?'

The staff nurse shook her head. 'Your first isn't due until two o'clock.'

'Which means you've twenty minutes free, and who better to spend them with than yours truly?' Jack declared as he swung into the staff room.

'Frankly I'd prefer a cup of tea if there's one left,' Peggie observed, reaching for the teapot.

'The girl wants tea instead of me.' The anaesthetist sighed mournfully. 'I'm shattered, distraught, I'm—'

'An idiot!' Peggie chuckled as Sally's eyes rolled heavenwards.

'Is there no end to this woman's heartlessness?' Jack protested. 'I offer her my heart, my soul—and she laughs at me. Now, if I'd been Gareth Davies...'

All amusement disappeared from Peggie's face. 'That's not funny, Jack.'

'But he's been a completely changed man since you came into our lives, sweet Peggie,' he declared. 'How did you manage it? Did you kiss the Blarney stone before you came to London?'

'I'll fly over to Ireland and bring it back and hit you over the head with it if you don't stop this foolishness,' she exclaimed, beginning to get really angry.

'O-ooh, so our Irish colleen has a temper, does she?' He grinned. 'Our Irish colleen...' He came to a halt and slapped his hand across his forehead. 'I've got it!'

'I suggest you keep it to yourself,' she retorted.

'No, listen,' he insisted. 'It's been driving me crazy for ages but I knew there was a song with your name in it, and it's just come to me.'

'A song...?'

'"If she's talking all the time, that's Peggie O'Neill,"' Jack sang at the top of his voice.

'Jack, keep your voice down,' she protested, well aware his deep baritone must be carrying all the way down the corridor, but he ignored her.

'"If she's smiling all the time,"' he continued, '"that's Peggie O'Neill. If she walks with a cute little walk, If she talks with a cute little talk, Full of vitality, great personality, That's Peggie O'Neill!"'

'You made that up!' Peggie exclaimed, breaking into laughter.

'I didn't—scout's honour. It really is a song, and—'

'And this is neither a music hall nor some cheap karaoke night in your local pub where you can sing it!' Gareth thundered, throwing open the staff room door without warning. 'This is a plastic surgery unit, and if none of you has anything better to do than sing stupid songs, perhaps it's time I took a closer look at my staffing requirements!'

A deathly hush descended on the staff room as he turned on his heel and strode away, then Jack smiled ruefully. 'Looks like the cease-fire's over, folks.'

'I thought it was too good to last,' Sally grumbled, but Peggie didn't say anything.

Jack and Sally might believe Gareth had merely reverted to type but she knew it wasn't as simple as that. Something more than the anaesthetist's singing had provoked Gareth's outburst, and as she made her way along to her consulting room she wished she could rid herself of the uncomfortable feeling that it was her.

'What on earth's happened?' Daisy Swan, the unit's student nurse, exclaimed the minute she saw her. 'I just met the boss in the corridor and he almost bit my head off.'

'Time of the month, perhaps?' Peggie suggested, but Daisy didn't laugh, and when Gareth appeared for Charlotte Heath's four o'clock appointment the student nurse's nervousness was almost tangible.

Why, oh, why, couldn't Gareth be as good with his staff as he was with his patients? Peggie wondered as she watched him put Charlotte completely at her ease. He was even good with the parents—just the right amount of gentle firmness and understanding—but with his staff…

And yet he had been getting better—even Jack had admitted it.

'Your GP says your daughter was knocked off her bike two years ago, Mrs Heath,' Peggie observed as Gareth examined the little girl's face.

Charlotte's mother nodded. 'She broke her leg and the surgeon at our local hospital was more concerned about that than the cuts on her face. He stitched them, and said they'd heal fine, but as you can see…'

Peggie could see, only too clearly. Not only had the surgeon used sutures which were far too big, he'd also failed to remove all the dirt from the wounds in Charlotte's face and now it was tattooed into her skin.

'That's the third case of residual scarring I've seen from that hospital in less than a year,' Gareth exclaimed furiously as soon as Charlotte and her mother had gone. 'What the hell are they using for sutures up there—chicken-wire?'

'Is there really very little we can do?' Peggie asked, remembering the tears which had welled in Mrs Heath's eyes when he'd told her.

'We could try cutting the tattooing out,' he replied, throwing his stethoscope down on her desk with frustration, 'but all she'd be left with is other—albeit fainter—scars. And as for those suture marks…' he shook his head bitterly '…she'll be left with them for the rest of her life, and it's all so damned unnecessary!'

'Sorry to disturb you, Dr O'Neill,' Daisy declared, popping her head round the consulting room door and glancing nervously from her to Gareth, 'but your last patient's here. Gabriella Finlay—removal of stitches in her arm?'

'Show her in,' Peggie replied, fully expecting Gareth to go, but to her surprise he simply stayed where he was, his face like thunder.

Well, she could hardly ask him to leave, she decided. All she could hope was he might have calmed down a bit by the time she'd finished seeing Gabriella.

And he might well have calmed down if she hadn't needed to ask Daisy for another pair of scissors after removing only two of Gabriella's stitches.

'Another pair?' the student nurse repeated in surprise.

'I'm not surprised,' Gareth exclaimed, pulling the scissors out of Peggie's fingers and examining them. 'These wouldn't cut butter.'

Quickly Daisy glanced down at her tray of instruments, then up at him uncomfortably. 'I-I don't appear to have another pair that size, Mr Davies.'

'There's a sudden world shortage, is there?' he declared, his voice biting. 'Our department has suddenly become so poor we can only afford one set?'

'I—I'm sorry, Mr Davies. I didn't think we'd need—'

'You are not paid to think, Nurse Swan, you are paid to be efficient,' he snapped. 'If you can't—'

'A number eleven scalpel blade will do just fine, Daisy,' Peggie interrupted swiftly, and the student nurse handed it to her, visibly shaken.

She wasn't the only one, Peggie thought as she cut and removed the rest of the sutures, all too aware she could have cut the atmosphere in her room with the scalpel blade too.

What in the world had got into him? she wondered, shooting him a glance. Yes, the scissors hadn't been as sharp as they should have been, but to treat a member of his staff like that in front of a patient and her father was unforgivable.

'I'd have thought there were subtler ways of making your point,' she said the minute a very subdued Daisy had led Gabriella and her father outside.

'Those scissors were blunt,' he replied tersely.

'And that justifies making Daisy look stupid, does it?' she retorted.

She was right, it didn't, and he might well have admitted he'd behaved badly if she'd left it there, but she didn't.

'I know you're angry about Charlotte Heath's face,' she continued, completely unaware of his thoughts, 'and I guess Jack serenading me in the staff room hasn't exactly helped your temper, but…'

He didn't even hear the rest of what she said. The mere mention of the anaesthetist's name was enough to make him realise why he was so angry. It wasn't the scissors— though Daisy should have remembered to bring more pairs—and it wasn't even the unnecessary damage to Charlotte Heath's face.

It was the image he'd been plagued by all afternoon. The image of Jack making love to the fresh-faced girl sitting in front of him. The image of him holding her, touching her, entering her, and as the image re-surfaced all too graphically in his mind the anger he had been trying to contain all afternoon exploded.

'Don't you dare question how I run my department, Dr O'Neill!' he exclaimed, his voice a whiplash.

'I wasn't—'

'I will not be criticised or judged by somebody who if she is not very careful will shortly become an *ex* member of my staff,' he thundered. 'Do I make myself clear?'

All too clear, she thought unhappily, longing to yell back at him that he sure as heck needed somebody to criticise him but knowing full well she couldn't. With a curt nod she bent down to get her bag, fully intending to sweep out of the room with as much cold dignity as she could manage. And she would have done it too if an unexpected wave of giddiness hadn't had her grabbing frantically at the edge of her desk the minute she stood up.

'What is it—what's wrong?' he asked, concern immediately replacing the anger in his voice.

'N-nothing,' she stammered, wishing the room would stop spinning and his voice didn't sound so far away. 'I— I just feel a little dizzy, that's all.'

Quickly he pushed her back into her seat and forced her

head down between her knees. 'Don't move—don't try to speak,' he ordered as she tried to do both. 'Just take slow, deep breaths, and tell me when the giddiness has passed.'

She did exactly as he said—she could hardly do anything else, she thought wryly, with two large hands clamped firmly on her shoulders.

Slowly—far too slowly for comfort—the room gradually stopped spinning and gingerly she raised her head to find him sitting back on his heels studying her.

'Is this the first time this has happened?' he demanded.

She shook her head and wished she hadn't. 'I—I've had one or two dizzy turns over the past fortnight,' she managed to reply, 'but nothing like as bad as this.'

He stared at her thoughtfully for a moment, then his dark eyebrows snapped down. 'Are you pregnant?'

Hot fiery colour replaced the white in her cheeks. 'Of course I'm not pregnant—I couldn't possibly be pregnant!'

For a second she almost thought she saw relief in his eyes before a frown darkened them. 'Any other symptoms—shortness of breath, heart palpitations?'

'No,' she insisted, longing only now to be gone. 'Look, I've probably just eaten something that's disagreed with me.'

It was the wrong thing to say. The puzzled look in his eyes vanished and he swore softly under his breath. 'You're on a diet, aren't you? That apple you had for lunch—you're on some damn fool diet because you think you need to lose some weight! God in heaven, there is absolutely nothing wrong with the way you look, and you sure as hell can't work the hours we do if you're starving yourself!'

'I'm not on a diet,' she protested, colouring faintly at the thought he might actually have bothered to look at her figure.

'Then what is it?' he exclaimed. 'People don't feel giddy for no reason.'

The colour on her cheeks darkened. She didn't want to

tell him—it was private, confidential—but she knew by the set of his jaw that he wasn't going to let it rest until she did.

'I haven't...I haven't maybe been eating as well as I should recently,' she said haltingly.

'Why ever not?' he demanded. 'You're in one of the hospital's self-catering flats, aren't you? You can cook whatever you want.'

She twisted her hands uncomfortably in her lap and her voice when she spoke was so low he had to bend his head to hear her.

'I know I can but, you see, everybody at home depends on the money I send. My parents—they're not rich people—and the farm hasn't been doing very well lately. Mary and Sinead can't help because they're still at school, and Connor's just started his apprenticeship with the local garage, and Patrick— He's finding it very hard to get a job. I send them what I can, but things in London—they're so expensive—and I had to pay a month's rent in advance for my flat, and then the plane fare here...'

Her voice trailed away into mortified silence and he cursed himself inwardly.

He should have realised. The pinched look about her face, the clothes she wore which, though neat and clean, were quite plainly not new. She was economising the only way she knew how to send money to her family—on food.

'Why didn't you tell me?' he said gently.

'It's my problem—not yours,' she murmured, unable to meet his gaze. 'And everything will be all right next week—I get paid then.'

'And how are you going to manage until next week?' He shook his head and reached into his pocket. 'I'll loan you some money.'

Her head came up, horror plain on her face. 'I couldn't possibly take money from you—it wouldn't be right!'

'Neither is starving yourself to death. Look, call it insurance,' he continued as she started to protest. 'The last thing I want is you fainting all over our patients, or making a mistake in theatre because you're ill from lack of food.'

Quickly he took out his wallet but when he extracted four fifty-pound notes she looked even more horrified.

'I couldn't possibly take all that—it would take me months to repay you!'

'So I'll wait months—or, better yet, why don't you just accept it as a gift?' he declared.

She shook her head vehemently. 'If…if I borrow money from you I'd have to pay it back. I couldn't look you in the face if I didn't.'

'Peggie—'

'W-would repaying it at twenty pounds a week be acceptable?'

He didn't know whether to laugh or cry. Twenty pounds was chicken-feed to him, but to her…

'Make it ten—it's an easier figure to remember,' he said quickly, but she looked so relieved that he couldn't prevent a small chuckle escaping his lips. 'You're a funny little thing, aren't you? How old are you?'

'Twenty four—I'll be twenty five in June.'

'You seem a lot younger,' he observed.

She sat up straighter in her seat. 'It's because I'm short. People always think you're younger if you're not very tall.'

'No, it isn't that,' he murmured.

He thought her naive, she realised unhappily, immature. Well, she supposed she was compared to all the other women he knew. Not that he knew that many if Sally was to be believed, but she was certain they would all have handled this situation a whole lot better than she was doing.

'What's wrong?' he asked as she stared miserably at the floor.

'Nothing,' she muttered.

To her surprise he leant forward, cupped her chin in his

hand, and forced her to look up at him. 'Come on—tell me.'

She couldn't have told him anything if she'd tried. In fact her heart was suddenly racing so fast that if she'd recorded it on a patient she'd have been pressing the panic button for the cardiac team.

And all because he was holding her chin in his hand.

It didn't make any sense, she told herself in confusion. He'd been closer to her in the operating theatre. Dammit, they'd practically been shoulder to shoulder in the operating theatre—well, shoulder to broad chest, to be exact— but this—this was different.

This time she wasn't thinking about his aftershave, or his smile, or the colour of his eyes. This time she was finding it very hard to think about anything at all apart from the disturbing sensations that his fingers seemed to be awakening deep inside her.

Her throat felt dry, tight, and she ran her tongue along her lips to moisten them and saw something flare in his eyes.

'Peggie…'

His voice was low, husky, and a shiver ran down her back.

The gap between them was narrowing—she knew it was. She could feel his breath warm against her cheek, could see his chest rising and falling rapidly in time to her own. Was he going to kiss her? His lips were certainly coming closer and involuntarily she tilted her head back to receive them, and…

'Um—right. Ten pounds a week—starting next Friday?' he declared, standing up abruptly, his cheeks dark with colour.

'F-Friday?' she stuttered, desperately grappling with her scattered wits as he walked quickly towards the door. 'Y-yes, of course. Fine.'

'Good—good.' He nodded, looking everywhere but at her. 'Right—fine—that's settled.'

'Gareth—'

He'd already gone. He'd just thrown open the door and walked away without a backward glance and all she could do was stare after him in breathless, bewildered confusion.

Chapter Four

'I'M NOT criticising you—please don't think that, Dr
O'Neill,' Mrs Turner declared nervously. 'But Kate's
face—the port wine stain—I thought—I hoped—it would
look an awful lot better than it does.'

'I did explain it would probably need three or four ses-
sions before we'd see any definite improvement,' Peggie
said gently. 'What the laser does, you see, is emit a pulse
of energy into the abnormal distribution of blood cells
which have caused Kate's haemangioma. The more pulses
of energy we give, the more cells are destroyed, and eventually the port-wine stain should disappear.'

'You mean it might not?' Mrs Turner said in clear dismay. 'I don't care one bit for myself, but Kate—'

'I think there's every likelihood you won't even know
she's had a port-wine stain by the time we're finished,'
Peggie said reassuringly. 'And now, young lady,' she continued, turning to Kate who had been happily absorbed in
the picture book Angel Matibele was showing her, 'are you
ready for your next treatment?'

The girl looked up and nodded. 'It's the same as last
time, isn't it? I have to wear goggles like when I go swim-
ming?'

'That's right.' Peggie smiled. 'Once the goggles are on
all you have to do is sit as still as you can while I shine
something which is a little bit like a torch at your cheek.'

It didn't take long to administer the second course of
treatment, or to make Kate another appointment for the
middle of July, and soon Peggie was busily collating and
filing the paperwork which had accumulated from her
morning clinic.

Or rather she was trying very hard to collate and file it, but eventually she threw down her pen and walked over to the window.

How long had it been since that heart-stopping moment when she'd thought Gareth was going to kiss her? Two weeks, one day, and nineteen hours ago—that was how long it had been.

Stop it, she told herself, closing her eyes and wrapping her arms tightly across her chest, just stop it. You've been over this a million damn times and you still don't know whether he was really going to kiss you or not. He probably had no intention of kissing you. It's probably all in your sad, pathetic little mind.

'And it probably is,' she murmured, opening her eyes and gazing down unhappily at the daffodils swaying gently in their tubs outside the hospital, 'because, let's face it, when it comes to men, your track record makes Snow White look experienced.'

And whose fault is that? she asked herself. It was your decision to keep every man at arm's length because you didn't want anything or anyone to distract you from your aim of becoming a doctor, and what have you got to show for it?

You're probably the only twenty-four-year-old virgin living in London, and you're most definitely the only twenty-four-year-old who can't make up her mind whether a man had been going to kiss you or not.

'Who says I wanted him to kiss me anyway?' she asked the sparrow perched on her window sill enjoying the crumbs she'd put out.

Oh, you wanted him to kiss you, he seemed to reply as he cocked his head to one side and gazed at her. You wanted him to do an awful lot more than just kiss you.

Then thank God it didn't happen, she told herself. Junior doctors and nurses were always falling for their boss. They had a brief affair and when it fizzled out their working relationship became a nightmare.

And what did she really know about him anyway? He might be the worst rat in the world. He might be the most unfeeling, self-absorbed man who'd ever walked Lizzie's corridors. I don't care if he is, her treacherous heart whispered, I honestly don't care.

With a sigh she turned from the window and grimaced at the sight of the paperwork still undone. Later, she thought, I'll do it later, and quickly went out into the corridor, only to dodge swiftly back into her consulting room again when she saw Gareth deep in conversation with Daisy.

This is ridiculous, she told herself. You're behaving like some second-rate actress in a B spy movie and all because you don't want to talk to the man. What's he going to say to you? Nothing. What's he going to do? Nothing. Because nothing happened, you idiot.

And yet still she waited until Gareth had gone before she came out of her room.

'Problems, Daisy?' she asked, seeing the student nurse's unhappy face.

'It's God—Mr Davies, I mean,' she said, glancing guiltily over her shoulder as though expecting him to suddenly reappear. 'He's driving me mad.'

'But I thought everything was sorted out?' Peggie exclaimed. 'He apologised to you about the scissors—'

'Yes, but every time he sees me now he keeps asking if I'm OK—if I've got any problems—and it's driving me crazy.'

'But—'

'I know, I know,' the student nurse said ruefully. 'I shouldn't be looking a gift horse in the mouth, but I just can't stand any more of this kindness. It's like having your crotchety old uncle suddenly becoming kind—you keep wondering when he's going to hit you.'

Peggie could not help but laugh. 'If you want my advice, enjoy it while it lasts.'

'That's easy for you to say.' Daisy groaned. 'You're not being driven nuts with kindness.'

And Peggie laughed again, but her laughter faded as she made her way down to IC.

She would have appreciated a little TLC at the moment. She would have preferred even more for that whole unsettling episode in her room never to have taken place.

Not that Gareth had ever referred to it—good grief, why should he?—and nor had he commented on the ten pounds she'd left in an envelope on his desk on Friday. In fact, apart from Peggie once or twice catching his eyes on her, his expression curiously pensive, he was his normal self. Well, perhaps not quite his normal self, she amended. To her he seemed a little quiet, a little withdrawn, perhaps even a little depressed.

'Back again?' Sam Harrison grinned when she appeared at the reception desk in IC. 'You're becoming quite a regular, aren't you?'

'Sorry,' she said with a laugh, 'but I promised Jonah I'd bring him some football magazines and as I'm free until after lunch I thought I'd bring them down now.'

The consultant gazed at her thoughtfully. 'You're becoming really fond of him, aren't you?'

Her smile became a little rueful. 'I know it's wrong to have favourites,' she admitted, 'but he's such a cutey, and so very brave.'

'Just don't get too fond of him, OK?' Sam observed. 'If anything should happen...'

'It won't,' she declared. 'The grafts Gareth and I applied to his arms are healing really well, and the ones Gareth and Tom did on his hands haven't been rejected.'

'No, but his heart rate's still all over the place, and the grafts on his arms have started to become very itchy.'

'Which is surely a good sign?' she argued. 'It usually means the dermis is starting to heal.'

'Or that we're going to end up with hypertrophic scarring—or keloids.'

Peggie gazed at Sam Harrison in dismay. The thought of Jonah developing hypertrophic scarring—permanent ugly red weals where a surgical incision had been made—was bad enough, but keloids could assume the proportions of grotesque tumours.

'You see what I mean about getting too fond of him?' the consultant said gently, watching her face. 'I'm not saying you shouldn't care—God forbid we should ever become cold, unemotional machines—but don't care too much, Peggie, or you'll end up being no help to your patients and crucifying yourself if anything goes wrong.'

'Nothing will go wrong,' she said firmly. 'Jonah will be fine—I just know he will.'

For a moment Sam Harrison gazed at her uncertainly, then smiled. 'I'm sure he will too if you and Gareth keep on visiting him like this.'

'Gareth's here?' she said, her heart sinking.

'He was reading to Jonah the last time I looked. Look, I'm sure he won't mind if you join him,' he continued, clearly sensing her indecision. 'In fact, to be honest I think he could do with some cheering up.'

So it hadn't been her imagination. Something *was* bothering Gareth but she doubted very much whether she would ever discover what it was. In fact, the likelihood of Gareth Davies unburdening his soul to her was about as probable as Jack Reid turning up to work tomorrow in a plain navy blue tie.

'So, are you going to join him?' Sam asked. 'Gareth, I mean?'

She had to. Common sense told her she couldn't hide round corners and skulk behind doors for the rest of her life. She was a fully qualified doctor, for goodness' sake, not a sixteen-year-old in the throws of her first crush, and it was high time she started acting like the professional she was supposed to be.

'Of course I am,' she declared firmly, making her way to the changing room.

But she had only just slipped her protective gown over her skirt and sweater and tied the tapes when the changing room door opened.

'Something wrong in Plastics?' Gareth exclaimed when he saw her, concern appearing instantly on his face.

'No—nothing,' she replied. 'I just came down to bring Jonah some magazines, that's all.'

'I'm afraid he's asleep.'

'It doesn't matter,' she said, wishing he would stop staring at her in that curiously blank fashion. 'I can leave them with Sister Gilbert and he can get them later. Sam says you're worried about Jonah developing keloids?' she continued as she began untying her gown.

'I'm afraid there's a very strong possibility.'

'But if there's a very strong possibility, can't you do something about it?' she protested.

'Unfortunately we don't know enough about what causes them to do anything,' he replied.

'But—'

'Peggie, we know a potential keloid developer is likely to be young, black, and has undergone full thickness grafting,' he continued, seeing her bewilderment. 'We know, too, that certain sites—like the upper arm, the shoulder, and breastbone—are more likely to produce a keloid—but what we don't know is why some patients' scars become hypertrophic and then keloid, and yet other at-risk patients sail through their operations with no trouble at all.'

'Couldn't you just remove the keloid surgically if one developed?'

He shook his head as he took off his gown. 'All that's likely to happen is a fresh keloid would develop.'

'So there's nothing we can do but wait and hope,' she murmured unhappily.

'That's about the size of it, yes,' he replied.

He wished he could tell her otherwise. He wished he had the nerve to put his arm round her shoulder and give her a comforting hug because it was clearly what she needed right now, but he knew he could do neither. Just seeing her unhappy face was a severe enough test of his will-power, and if he actually touched her…

Why did she have to have this effect on him? he wondered, running some cold water quickly into the sink. Lord, he still broke out in a sweat at the thought of how close he'd come to kissing her that afternoon, and if he had…

Getting involved with somebody who worked at the hospital was asking for trouble. Getting involved with somebody who worked for him was a recipe for disaster. Marianne had taught him that, and though making love to Peggie might have alleviated the physical ache he felt whenever she was near, it wouldn't have solved anything, and it sure as heck wouldn't have changed anything either, he thought bitterly.

'I'm sorry, but do you think you could give me a hand?'

'A hand?' he repeated, turning to find her wrestling with the neck of her gown, her face flushed.

'These damn ties have got knotted and I can't get them undone.'

'No problem,' he declared heartily, too heartily. 'Turn round and I'll soon get you out of it.'

It was an unfortunate choice of words, he decided as she obediently turned her back to him. He wanted to get her out of an awful lot more than just her protective gown. He wanted to find out whether the fullness of her breasts was as real as he kept imagining, and if the glorious curve of her hips would mould to his hands as he had so often dreamt they would.

'Perhaps we should just cut it off?' she murmured as he bit back a groan.

It would certainly solve his current problem permanently, he thought ruefully. And he definitely needed something to solve it, he realised as she lifted her hair higher off the back of her neck and he experienced an overwhelming urge to plant a row of kisses along the smooth soft skin she had exposed. If he didn't, he was going to go nuts.

'All done,' he exclaimed, pulling the tapes free with more vigour than finesse. 'And now, you'll have to excuse me,' he continued, stepping back from her quickly. 'I'm due in Orthopaedics to assess the sort of reconstructive surgery a twelve-year-old boy with a fractured lower tibia is going to need.'

'Can I come with you? I'm free until Robbie Taylor's rhinoplasty this afternoon, you see,' she added hurriedly as his eyebrows lowered slightly, 'and I'd like to observe, if you don't mind.'

He wanted to say no. He wanted to say half an hour in her company was about as much as his frayed nerves could stand, but she was his SHO and he knew it was important for her to learn.

Try thinking of her as a twenty-four-year-old bloke with acne, his mind advised—that should put a damper on your damned libido. If only it were that easy, he thought, biting back another groan as a wide smile lit up her face when he nodded reluctantly. If only it were that simple.

'You said the boy you're going to see has a fractured lower tibia?' she said as she accompanied him out of Intensive Care.

'He was brought into A and E two days ago having been knocked down by a car,' he replied, keeping his gaze fixed very firmly ahead. 'Unfortunately the car dragged him along the road and his leg is very badly flayed.'

She grimaced. 'Sounds tricky.'

'It could be if there's extensive muscle damage but I'm

hoping simple split-skin grafts might be enough. Lucas
Morrison phoned me as soon as the boy came in so there
shouldn't be any problem if I do need to take some grafts.'

'Why might there be problems?' she asked, puzzled.

'Think about it, Peggie. If Lucas had used plaster of Paris
to immobilise the fracture—'

'It would have been virtually impossible for you to reach
the skin unless you cut a very large window in the cast
which would affect the setting of the fracture,' she finished
for him with dawning understanding. 'Would it have been
all right if he'd used an internal fixation using plates and
screws?'

He shook his head. 'There would be too much soft tissue
damage. The best way to keep the fracture immobile, and
yet also allow us to apply any skin grafts, is to use the
external fixation frame.'

'In other words, it's very important to keep on good
terms with Orthopaedics,' she observed.

'It's vitally important.'

'And are you always on good terms with them?' she
could not resist asking with an impish smile.

He didn't smile back. All he said as he pushed open the
door of Orthopaedics was, 'Lucas Morrison and I understand one another.'

Well, lucky old Lucas, she thought with a sigh as the
orthopaedic consultant walked towards them.

'Right on time as usual, Gareth,' he exclaimed. 'Paul's
ready for you but I'm afraid he's pretty grumpy. I'll rustle
up one of my staff—'

'No need,' Gareth interrupted. 'I've got my SHO, Peggie
O'Neill, with me this morning.'

Lucas Morrison smiled at her and Peggie smiled back.
If the rumours currently flying around the hospital were true
the orthopaedic surgeon was in love with Claudia Craven,
a junior doctor on his staff. And if the rumour factory was

equally to be believed, things weren't going well between them.

Which only goes to prove how sensible it is not to get involved with someone you work with, Peggie told herself as she followed Gareth down the ward, and heartily wished she could make herself believe it.

'Oh, for God's sake can't you people just leave me alone?' Paul Marshall groaned when he saw them. 'I'm fed up with being prodded and poked about.'

'This won't take long, I promise.' Gareth smiled. 'I only want to take a little look at your leg.'

'That's what the last bloke said and see the result,' the boy retorted, gazing down with some distaste at the metal rods protruding from his leg.

'Looking like something out of a horror movie,' Peggie observed, her eyes dancing, and Paul gave an involuntary chuckle.

It was clear even to her that Gareth wasn't going to get away with a simple split-skin graft. Not only had Paul's leg been very badly flayed because of contact with a pneumatic tyre, it also looked very much as though there was damage to the muscle. The muscle fibres were much darker than they should have been, and when Gareth pinched them they didn't contract at all.

'It looks like you're going to have to make a trip to the theatre, Paul,' Gareth declared.

'But I thought— That Morrison bloke said you'd probably just give me a local anaesthetic and shave bits of skin off me,' the boy protested.

'An ordinary skin graft isn't going to be of much use to you, I'm afraid,' Gareth said gently. 'I need to transfer some of your muscle as well as your skin, and for that you'll need to be anaesthetised with a general anaesthetic.'

'You mean I'll be asleep?' the boy replied, clear relief appearing in his eyes for a second, then he shrugged airily.

'Suits me fine. I thought lying about while you cut bits of skin off me sounded kinda boring anyway.'

'It can be.' Gareth nodded, recognising the fear behind the bravado. 'See you Thursday, Paul.'

'Yeah, right. If I've nothing better to do,' he answered dismissively, and Peggie could not help but chuckle as Gareth led the way back down the ward.

'The poor soul's terrified witless but damned if he's going to let anybody know it.'

'Everyone deals with fear in their own way,' Gareth replied. 'Some children withdraw, some children—'

'I *thought* I recognised those dulcet Welsh tones.' A husky feminine voice laughed. 'Where in the world have you been hiding yourself lately, you naughty man?'

Peggie turned quickly to see who had spoken and her jaw dropped.

'Peggie, I don't think you've met Frances Harper—Assistant Senior Physiotherapist at Lizzie's,' Gareth declared with a tight smile. 'Frances, this is my new SHO, Peggie O'Neill.'

'*You're* Peggie O'Neill?' Frances gasped, her eyes absorbing Peggie's plain black skirt and equally simple rollnecked red sweater. 'But I thought…' She gave a tinkling little laugh. 'Oh, my goodness, I thought you were somebody's daughter here on work experience.'

Bitch, Peggie thought savagely, amazed at the surge of animosity that rose in her breast. Beautiful, designer-clad, eight-stone bitch.

And Frances Harper was beautiful. Long blonde hair perfectly sculptured into a sleek chignon, limpid cornflower-blue eyes, a pair of impossibly long legs, and a figure which would make you give up chocolates for life. If Gareth wasn't interested in a girl who looked like this, she thought sadly, what hope was there he'd look twice at somebody like her?

'I'm so glad I ran into you, Gary,' Frances exclaimed,

turning back to him with a dazzling smile, 'because I noticed Covent Garden is staging *Tosca* this Saturday.'

Gary? She called him *Gary?* Peggie crushed down the bubble of laughter that welled within her with difficulty.

'I remembered you said it was one of your favourite operas,' Frances continued, 'and I think I can get two tickets—'

'Sorry, Frances,' he interrupted as his bleeper sounded, though in truth Peggie thought he actually looked secretly relieved as he strode to the phone, and he was back within seconds. 'We're needed in theatre, Peggie. Nine-year-old on her way up from A and E. Apparently she's lost the top quarter of her ear and it's too ragged for them to be able to stitch it back on again.'

'You'll remember to let me know about those tickets, won't you, Gary?' Frances called after him as he made for the door.

Peggie heard him mutter something in reply but it didn't sound very much like, 'See you in Covent Garden, Frances,' and a small smile curved her lips as they hurried to the operating theatre. OK, so he'd never be interested in her in a million years, but at least it looked as though The Siren was going to be equally unlucky.

'What's the situation, Jack?' Gareth asked when they arrived.

'Patient's name is Wendy Arnold. Apparently she got into a fight with another girl at school, things got a bit nasty, and the girl bit the top of her ear off.'

'A *girl* bit it off?' Peggie gasped in horror.

'Oh, you'd be surprised at what the female of the species can do,' Gareth observed, his lip curling. 'In fact, when it comes to out-and-out viciousness, women come top of the league every time.'

'Is that the voice of experience speaking, boss?' Jack grinned, but Gareth didn't answer. He merely walked into one of the changing cubicles and slammed the door shut.

It was the voice of experience talking, he thought, quickly stripping off his clothes. The voice of experience which made this fixation he had with Peggie O'Neill all the more ridiculous.

He had to get the situation under control. He had to get himself under control, or he could see nothing but pain and heartbreak ahead for both of them. God in heaven, it shouldn't be too difficult for a man of his intelligence to be polite but distant, but the minute he opened the cubicle door he realised it was going to be damn near impossible.

Peggie wasn't quite ready. She was still busily piling her hair up under her cap and he wouldn't have believed how erotic such a simple act could be. For a second he gazed at her, his eyes taking in the slender curve of her neck, the way her breasts strained against her theatre top as she raised her arms, but when she turned and caught sight of him staring at her guilt flooded through him.

'For God's sake get a move on, Peggie,' he snapped, taking refuge in anger. 'We haven't got all day!'

Quickly she thrust the remainder of her hair under her cap, clearly considerably flustered. 'I'm ready.'

'About time, too,' he replied, pushing open the door into the theatre with his elbows, knowing he had sounded quite unbelievably petty, but totally unable to stop himself.

'BP normal, heartbeat steady,' Jack declared from his position by the operating table. 'All vital signs A OK, Gareth.'

'Blood, Sally?'

'Four units of cross-matched ready should you need them, Gareth.'

'Are you going to patch the ear with a skin graft?' Peggie said as she took her position beside him. 'Or take some cartilage from the chest area to act as scaffolding for a graft?'

'Neither,' he answered tightly, wishing she wouldn't stand quite so close. 'The ear wouldn't stand up as real ear should with a skin graft, and if I use cartilage from the chest the appearance won't be very much better and nor would she have any feeling in the reconstructed part.'

'So what are you going to do?' she asked.

'Use part of the remaining ear—the conical section where a glasses arm would sit—strip it back, and swing it up over the defect, putting both cartilage and skin into place.'

'But won't you need to be able to identify the blood supply to the ear and the surrounding tissue to do that?' she exclaimed.

'And you don't think I can?' he declared, his voice suddenly ice-cold.

'No—I mean, yes, I-I'm sure you can,' she stammered, well aware that Jack and Sally were looking at Gareth in puzzled astonishment. 'I didn't mean…I only meant…I'm sorry—I shouldn't have said anything.'

And she wished with all her heart that she hadn't as he began the extremely difficult job of identifying the blood supply. She truly hadn't intended to imply a lack of faith in his ability, only admiration for his skill in attempting something so radical, but his set expression and the curt way he answered her every question while he performed the operation told her he would never believe her.

'Boy, but somebody surely got out of bed on the wrong side this morning,' Sally observed dryly when the operation was over and Gareth had gone out to the reception area to see if Robbie Taylor had arrived for his rhinoplasty.

'Now that's not a problem I ever have, my lovely.' Jack grinned. 'A fact you could verify yourself if you'd care to sample the overnight hospitality of number 21 Crown Circus.'

'In your dreams, Jack,' she scoffed. 'I'd have to be kidnapped and bound hand and foot before I'd ever set foot in your flat.'

'Sounds good to me,' he exclaimed, his eyes sparkling.

'You're sick—you know that, don't you?' the staff nurse replied as she stripped the protective cover off the operating table before opening the sterile drawer to retrieve the instruments Gareth would need for his operation on Robbie Taylor.

'Heart-sick.' The anaesthetist sighed, slumping dramatically over his heart machine. 'Every day you cut me to the quick, every day you pierce my heart with your cruel barbs—'

'It's a pity I couldn't pierce that over-inflated ego of yours,' she countered, her eyes dancing.

'But, Sall, my lovely, Sall, my beautiful—'

'Save your speeches for somebody with nothing between her ears,' she interrupted. 'Now stop fooling about,' she added with a warning glance. 'God's coming.'

'I bet you didn't know one of the earliest known rhinoplasty ops was performed in Italy in the sixteenth century by a man called Gaspare Tagliacozzi on a man who'd lost his nose through syphilis?' Jack commented, apparently completely unperturbed by Gareth's reappearance.

'Did it work?' Peggie could not help but ask in amazement.

'According to his journals it did. He partially detached a piece of skin from the upper arm of his patient and waited until it had established itself as a viable tissue before stitching it to the remains of his nose.'

'You mean the poor man had to walk around with his arm stitched to his nose!' She laughed.

'He did—for fourteen days, in fact. It took Tagliacozzi five months to reshape the flap into a new nose.'

'And if we don't get this operation started soon it may well take us five months to complete it,' Gareth declared tersely.

The operation to repair Robbie Taylor's nose was completed in virtual silence. Luckily the damage caused to it when he'd been hit by a cricket bat didn't require a cartilage graft and Gareth was able to reconstruct his nose by making internal incisions, but Peggie still felt totally wrung out by the time it was over.

Would she ever figure out what made Gareth Davies tick? she wondered as she watched him slam out of the changing room without a word. More to the point, would she ever be able to watch him work again and not remember the gentle feel of his hands under her chin and their touch against the back of her neck?

And that was all her own damn fault. She should never have asked him for help with those tapes. She should just have got a pair of scissors and cut them free but now she was going to have another unsettling memory to plague her, another disturbing memory to haunt her dreams. And for what? Nothing. Absolutely nothing at all.

'Cheer up, love.'

She jumped at the sound of the unexpected voice and turned to find Jack gazing at her, his face sympathetic.

'I am cheerful,' she replied, forcing a smile to her lips. 'I'm just a bit tired, that's all.'

'Tired be damned, Peggie,' he observed. 'You're falling for the boss, aren't you?'

'Of course I'm not,' she exclaimed, all too aware that the colour on her cheeks was totally contradicting her words. 'What on earth gave you such a ridiculous idea?'

'Peggie, I've got ears and I've got eyes, and if ever a girl's smitten it's you. And I'd say good luck to you if I thought you stood a cat in hell's chance of making it work,' he continued as she tried to protest, 'but I've worked for Gareth for almost two years now and in all that time he's never dated anyone either in or out of the hospital. His work is everything to him—there's no room in it for personal relationships.'

'Just as well I'm not looking for one, then, isn't it?' she managed to reply and knew that Jack wasn't for one minute deceived. 'And what about you?' she continued quickly.

'All this teasing and squabbling you do with Sally—you really like her, don't you?'

'I like women, full stop.' He laughed.

She didn't believe him. There'd been times when she'd caught his gaze on Sally, a little wistful, a little sad, and sometimes she'd even found herself thinking that for all his talk Jack was actually rather lonely.

'Where are you from originally, Jack?' she asked. 'Your accent—it's not a London one.'

'I be from deepest Somerset, me dear, me darlin',' he replied in a mock country yokel accent, and she shook her head at him.

'Aren't you ever serious?'

'Life's too short, Peggie.'

'Even to be yourself?'

He stared at her silently for a moment, then a small smile curved his lips. 'You're too quick by half, Peggie O'Neill.'

'I think Sally would like you—more than like you—if you'd only let her see the real you,' she said gently.

His smile became distinctly crooked. 'Maybe she would, maybe pigs do fly, and maybe the moon really is made of green cheese.'

'Jack—'

'You know, you never did take me up on that rain check for dinner,' he continued quickly. 'What about my place tonight—a candlelit dinner for two—overnight stay optional?'

And as she laughed and shook her head she could not help but think that maybe she and Jack Reid had an awful lot more in common than she would ever have imagined.

Chapter Five

'BP AND heart rate, Jack?'

'Fine, Peggie. No worries at all.'

'Units of cross match available if I need them, Sally?'

'On stand-by, Peggie.'

'This poor little chap's ears certainly do need pinning back,' Tom Kerr declared, gazing down at Billy Oswald who was fast asleep on the operating table. 'I can just imagine the kind of taunts he's had to endure at school. Cab ears and elephant boy were probably the kindest.'

'Children can be very cruel at times,' Peggie observed, selecting a scalpel from the tray of instruments Sally was holding out to her.

'Tell me about it.' The specialist registrar grimaced. 'My daughter's best friend isn't her best friend any more and you'd think the end of the world had come.'

'How old is your daughter?' Peggie asked, carefully removing a strip of skin from behind Billy's ear to expose the cartilage she was going to remodel.

'Almost five.'

'And at that age everything is either a major triumph or a major catastrophe. There's never any middle ground.'

'My wife says they'll probably be the best of friends again in a week, but quite frankly I don't think I'll survive 'til then.'

'It's called the joys of parenthood, Tom.' Peggie laughed.

'I'll try and remember that,' he said wryly. 'How's the cartilage coming on?' he added, leaning forward to take a closer look.

'Good, I think. Does it look OK to you?'

'You're the one doing the otoplasty, not me.' He smiled. 'If you think it's fine, it's fine.'

Peggie gazed down at the cartilage she'd been working on and nodded. 'It's fine.'

'Then all you have to do is stitch the two edges of the wound together, pulling the ear closer to the head, then you can tackle his left ear.'

It was so restful operating with Tom. He never raised his voice, never got into a flap. OK, so he might not possess Gareth's spectacular surgical skills, but after enduring Gareth's unpredictable temper for the last five days Peggie felt she'd happily settle for some peace and quiet.

There was peace and quiet, however, and there was peace and quiet, and she had to concede that the operating theatre was quite unusually silent this morning. Normally Jack never shut up for a moment, but today he'd scarcely said a word, and there'd been none of his usual verbal sparring with Sally. And the staff nurse was remarkably quiet too, Peggie realised, shooting the girl a slightly puzzled glance.

Perhaps Jack had teased her once too often. Perhaps Sally had really lost her temper. Whatever had happened she just hoped they'd resolve their differences soon. Gareth in a bad temper was bad enough but if Sally and Jack joined him it would make operating a nightmare.

'Talking about Gareth—'

'Were we?' Tom interrupted, his eyes twinkling.

'No, but never mind.' She chuckled, fighting down the tide of colour she knew was staining her cheeks. 'Has he...would you happen to know whether he's ever had any facial surgery?'

'What on earth put that idea in your head?' the specialist registrar asked in surprise.

'I don't know,' she admitted. 'I just wondered—he's so very good with children like Billy—so defensive of their rights to have surgery—I wondered if he'd had some facial disfigurement himself?'

'I don't think you need to have suffered from something in order to empathise with other people's unhappiness, do you?' he remarked.

He was right, you didn't, but she still could not rid herself of the feeling that Gareth's anger when she'd commented about Billy Oswald's GP had possessed a personal element.

'Good work,' Tom observed when she had finished remoulding the cartilage in Billy's left ear and sutured it back against his head. 'You've done a really neat job there and the scars should be well hidden in the creases between his ears and scalp.'

'I just hope I haven't made the stitches too loose,' she said a little uncertainly as Sally and Jack wheeled the child out into Recovery and she and Tom returned to the changing room. 'The last thing I want is the ears springing back, but if I'd made them too tight—'

'Relax, Peggie,' Tom said gently. 'You did a super job and not even Gareth could find anything to criticise.'

'I bet he'll try, though,' she said ruefully as she pulled off her surgical gloves.

'I bet he will, too.' He laughed. 'Which reminds me,' he continued, glancing up at the changing-room clock, 'he's asked me to see a sales rep for him and if I don't appear he'll have my guts for garters.'

And he would too, Peggie thought as Tom disappeared out the door.

Nobody had been immune from Gareth's anger over the last few days and there had been times when she'd felt a seat on top of a rumbling volcano would have been preferable to working in the plastics unit.

'You look exactly how I feel.' Sally sighed as she came into the changing room.

Peggie chuckled, then cleared her throat. 'Look, tell me to mind my own business and I won't take offence. Tell me to keep my nose out of your affairs and I won't say another word, but sometimes a trouble shared really can be a trouble halved.'

The staff nurse pulled off her theatre cap and ran her hands through her short brown bob with a sigh. 'It's Jack. He's asked me out.'

'Again?' Peggie laughed but Sally didn't.

'I thought I knew him, Peggie,' she murmured. 'All the tricks he could play, all the flattery he could dish out, but the way he asked me—it was like being asked out by somebody I didn't know.'

'So what did you say?'

'That I'd think about it,' Sally said, her expression rueful. 'Honestly, Peggie, I need my head examined. I should just have turned him down flat like I normally do.'

'Maybe not. Maybe if you go out with him you'll be surprised—'

'Yeah, right—like when I'm fighting off Mr Octopus Hands it'll be a real big surprise, I don't think.'

'Sally—'

'What would you do, Peggie?'

'I'd go out with him. Not me, personally,' she added hurriedly in case Sally should think otherwise. 'I like Jack—I do—but not in that way, if you see what I mean.'

'You mean you'd really go out with a man even though all your instincts told you you'd probably end up getting hurt?' Sally said curiously.

A pair of deep green eyes floated into Peggie's mind and unconsciously her face softened. 'I'd risk it.'

Sally shook her head. 'Maybe I will go out with him— maybe what I really need is a brain transplant for even considering it.'

Maybe she needed a brain transplant too, Peggie decided as she walked slowly back to the plastics unit. Sally might think she had problems but at least she wasn't attracted to a man like Gareth. A man who could be unbelievably kind and generous one minute, and a thorough-going awkward sod the next.

And she was attracted to him. She could not call it love—how could she fall in love with a man she hardly knew?—but attracted.... If being attracted to someone meant your heart beat a little faster when he was near. If being attracted meant you felt unhappy and out of sorts all the time, then she was attracted, and she had it bad...real bad.

'Something up, David?' she asked as David Chang gasped with clear relief the minute she opened the door of the plastics unit.

'I've been trying to get hold of you for the last half-hour. God's got a meeting with a Mr & Mrs Docherty at three o'clock and he wants you to sit in.'

'Me?' she exclaimed. 'But—'

'Ours not to reason why, Peggie, but you'd better get a move on—it's five to three already.'

She nodded. The name Docherty meant nothing to her and if the case was a difficult one she'd have thought Tom was the logical choice to sit in, but, as David had said, hers was not to reason why.

'I was expecting you fifteen minutes ago,' Gareth declared when she opened his consulting room door.

'If I'd known you were expecting me, I'd have been here fifteen minutes ago,' she could not help but reply, her voice every bit as cool as his.

For a second he looked as though he was going to pursue the matter before clearly thinking the better of it. 'Liam Docherty, four years old, Down's syndrome child.'

'And his problem is?' she asked, sitting down.

'That is his problem.'

'I'm sorry, but I don't follow—'

'You will,' he interrupted as Angel Matibele ushered Liam and his parents in.

And she did. Liam Docherty was clearly a very loving

and lovable child. He was also just as clearly a Down's syndrome child with the sloping eyes, flat nose, wide cheeks and over-large tongue of a Down's sufferer, and it was these characteristics Mr & Mrs Docherty wanted changed.

'We read in the newspapers that it's possible for Liam to have his face altered so he'd look— Well, he'd look more normal,' Mr Docherty declared hesitantly.

'I can certainly change the way he looks.' Gareth nodded. 'I could build up his nose so it's not so flat, change the shape of his eyes so they don't slant the way they do, and re-contour his cheeks and chin. Some surgeons would recommend doing all these procedures in one operation but personally I'd prefer to alter one part of his face at a time. I think it's far less stressful for the child.'

'But it is possible?' Mrs Docherty declared.

'Yes, it is possible.'

Peggie sat in silence as the Dochertys discussed the various options open to them and when they'd gone Gareth turned to her, his eyebrows raised.

'When I asked you to sit in on the consultation I expected you to contribute something to the conversation.'

'There didn't seem a whole lot for me to say,' she murmured. 'The Dochertys asked their questions, you answered them. The ethics of what they were suggesting didn't seem to be on the agenda.'

'The ethics?' he repeated, his eyes fixed on her.

She opened her mouth, then closed it again. Judging on what had happened over the last few days when anyone had queried any of his decisions, she'd get her head in her hands if she said what she really thought. Oh, what the hell? she decided.

'This surgery for Liam Docherty,' she began. 'I know you can do it—I know you have the necessary skills to do it. What concerns me is whether you should be doing it at all.'

'You think I shouldn't?' he observed.

'I do,' she said firmly. 'Liam is a lovely little boy and in my opinion that's a lot more important than his outward appearance.'

Without a word of warning he caught hold of her wrist, pulled her out of her seat, and propelled her across to the mirror on his wall. 'Tell me what you see, Peggie.'

'Gareth—'

'Tell me what you see,' he insisted.

She stared at her reflection and sighed. 'I see a short, dumpy girl with a pair of brown eyes, a nose that's too small, a mouth that's too big, and a lot of black hair.'

'I could argue with you about that description,' he commented with a ghost of a smile, 'but I won't right now. What I'm trying to say is you look "normal". There are no blemishes on your face that would make people stare, no features which would make people pin a label on you even before you'd opened your mouth.'

'But if I were a Down's syndrome child and you changed my appearance I would still be a Down's syndrome child,' she argued. 'You couldn't "cure" me.'

'No, I couldn't, but I can alter the way society regards you. I can give you features which won't cause distaste wherever you go, a face which won't cause anyone else to make assumptions, judgements about you.'

'But what's so wrong about being different?' she protested. 'We should be encouraging society to accept that difference, not changing children so they fit in with what society regards as "normal".'

'I agree entirely,' he declared, 'and if I could change society I would, but I can't. All I can do is change the way one little boy looks and hopefully his life will be a little easier, the snubs and rejections he'll have to face as he gets older will be a little less.'

'But he'll still be a handicapped child,' she insisted. 'Nothing you can do can alter that.'

He raked his hands through his black hair. 'Peggie, I can only do what I can—nobody could do more.'

She shook her head. 'The point is nobody should have to do it all.'

'Peggie—'

'Why did you ask me to sit in with you?' she demanded. 'You know what's possible and what's not, and you'd already made up your mind before you saw the Dochertys that you were going to do what they wanted.'

'Idle curiosity, I suppose,' he murmured as he gazed down at her. 'I wondered how you'd react to their proposal.'

'You make it sound like I sat some kind of test,' she said in confusion.

'Maybe you did.'

'Gareth—'

'Paul Marshall's due in theatre in half an hour for his muscle and skin flap transference,' he interrupted abruptly. 'We'd better go.'

'We?' she repeated as he moved to the door. 'But I thought Tom and I were doing the op?'

'He's still stuck with the sales rep, so it's you and me and Bob Bremen.'

Poor Bob, Peggie thought. The student doctor meant well and tried even harder, but there was no denying he was a bundle of nerves and never performed well when Gareth was watching. All she could hope was Gareth would treat him gently, though on the evidence of the past few days it was a singularly feeble hope.

To her amazement, however, far from treating any of Bob's questions with scathing contempt, Gareth practically bent over backwards to be helpful.

'Deciding whether a damaged limb can ever be a useful functioning one *is* the most important consideration in a case like this.' He nodded when Bob tentatively put that point to him. 'Very severely injured limbs can be saved, but you've got to be realistic and face the possibility of amputation. Forceps and scissors, please, Sally.'

'And you're performing a skin-flap operation rather than a skin graft because of the muscle damage?' Bob said as Gareth selected the tiny instruments he was going to use.

'That's right,' Gareth replied. 'Suction catheter, Peggie. Unlike a skin graft, a skin flap retains its blood supply— either by remaining attached at one end to the donor site, or through reattachment of its blood vessels to vessels at the new site—which makes it very useful for covering an area that has lost its blood supply and where a graft wouldn't "take".'

'BP a little fast, Gareth, heart-rate normal.'

'Thanks, Jack. If you're lucky and the area to be covered is relatively small and there's sufficient skin nearby,' Gareth continued, 'the flap can be left attached at one end and moved by stretching, or rotating it.'

'And can you do that in Paul's case?' Bob asked, stepping nearer to get a closer look.

Gareth shook his head. 'The skin and muscle will have to be removed from another area of the body and its blood vessels attached to new arteries and veins at the site of the graft.'

'That sounds a hell of a job,' Bob exclaimed, then crimsoned as he realised what he had said.

At any time over the last few days such an ill-advised chance remark would have earned him an ear-blasting, but to everyone's surprise Gareth merely smiled and murmured, 'It ain't easy, that's for sure,' and a collective sigh of relief rippled round the theatre.

Whatever had caused Gareth's bad temper seemed to have gone and everyone could only hope it lasted.

The operation was a long, exhausting one. Not only did Gareth have to decide which donor area would give the best blood and muscle supply, he had also to find an artery and vein of the right size in Paul's damaged leg to which these could be joined.

And even then he wasn't finished. Because of the size of the skin flap, he had to take a split-skin graft from Paul's chest to cover the donor site.

'He's amazing, isn't he?' Bob Bremen declared in admiration when he and Peggie were back in the changing room and Gareth had gone through into Recovery with Paul. 'I mean, his skill, his ability...'

'It takes your breath away sometimes, doesn't it?' Peggie chuckled. 'I keep telling myself that with practice I might one day be as good as he is.'

Bob sighed. 'I don't think I'll ever be.'

'You've only just started,' she said encouragingly. 'You can't expect to have his expertise.'

'No, but I never imagined the work would be so stressful,' the junior doctor observed. 'I did three months with Ben Harvey down in General Medical and that was tough going, but Plastics... Plastics is something else.'

She'd never found it stressful. Challenging—yes. Rewarding—most definitely. But as she changed out of her theatre clothes and made her way down to IC, she knew she could never picture herself doing anything else.

'I know, I know—I'm back again—' she laughed as Sam Harrison stared at her blankly '—but I promised Jonah I'd bring down a book he wanted and I've only just got off duty.'

'Peggie...he isn't here.'

'You mean, you've moved him down to the surgical ward?' she exclaimed. 'Isn't that a bit soon? I'm not questioning your judgement—'

'Peggie, he died two hours ago.'

She stared uncomprehendingly at him for a moment, then shook her head. 'You must be thinking about somebody else. Jonah and I—we had this long discussion about his white mouse this morning and—'

'He had a massive cardiac arrest just after lunch,' Sam interrupted gently. 'We tried everything but we just couldn't save him.'

'Do…do you have any idea why it happened?' she asked through the hard lump wedged in her throat.

He shook his head. 'We won't know anything until we get the results from the autopsy. Look, come through to my office,' he continued, his face worried, concerned. 'I'll make you a cup of coffee—we can talk.'

About what? she wondered. About how medical science didn't have all the answers, how they weren't gods, and how Jonah couldn't have felt anything?

She didn't want to hear, she didn't want to hear any of it.

'Thanks for the offer, Sam,' she said quickly, 'but I have…I have to go.'

And somehow she made it out of the unit. Somehow she even managed to get halfway down the corridor before she realised she was crying.

Why did it have to be Jonah? her heart asked. Why, of all the children she had seen since she'd come to Lizzie's, did it have to be him?

A gulping sob came from her and she pressed her fist tightly against her mouth to quell the others she knew would surely follow. Go home, her brain urged. You're finished for the day, go home, but before she could move she heard the sound of running feet behind her.

Nobody must see her like this—she couldn't bear it if anybody saw her like this—and desperately she turned and stared at the notice board beside her, seeing none of the bright posters and announcements, hoping whoever it was would simply pass by, but they didn't.

The footsteps stopped behind her, and a familiar voice said softly, 'Peggie… Oh, Peggie, I just heard, and I'm so very, very sorry.'

'He was only five, Gareth,' she said, her voice breaking

as she turned to face him. 'He had his whole life ahead of him—and now…now…'

. She dashed her hand across her eyes but it didn't help. She was crying properly now—large hot tears which ran down her nose and into her mouth—and for a second Gareth patted her shoulder tentatively, then threw caution to the wind and drew her into his arms.

Dimly he realised he ought to have found the situation deeply embarrassing. She was a member of his staff, he was her boss, and the hospital rumour factory would have a field day if anyone saw them, but he didn't find it embarrassing. Her hair might be tickling his nose, his shirt might be growing steadily damper by the second, but it felt quite, quite wonderful.

'I'm sorry…I'm so sorry.' She hiccuped when her grief had spent itself. 'Crying all over you like this—'

'Don't be silly,' he murmured gruffly, not wanting her to move, not wanting to let go of the woman who seemed to fit so well into his arms. 'There's nothing to be sorry about.'

'I think…maybe I should go home,' she mumbled, extricating herself from his reluctant arms and blowing her nose vigorously.

'To what?' he demanded. 'To an empty flat—to an evening spent thinking about Jonah? Get your coat, Peggie—I'm taking you out to dinner.'

She shook her head. 'I wouldn't be any kind of company—'

'So we'll sit in silence.'

'Gareth, be sensible,' she protested. 'Not only would I be lousy company, my face must be all blotchy, my nose is bound to be red, and I'm wearing my oldest skirt and sweater.'

'So I'll find a very dark restaurant.'

She gave a hiccuping laugh. 'Gareth—'

'Get your coat, Peggie.'

*   *   *

The restaurant wasn't nearly as dark as Peggie would have wished. For a start she could still see the other diners and, more importantly, she knew they could see her.

'Relax,' Gareth observed as she sank further down into her seat in a vain attempt to blend with the art nouveau decor. 'You look fine.'

She didn't look fine. She could tell very well that she didn't look fine by the very definite sniff the obsequious waiter gave as he took their order.

'Do you come here a lot?' she asked, determinedly resisting the impulse to slide even further down in her seat.

'Occasionally,' he replied dismissively. 'It's far enough away from the hospital to ensure I don't run into any colleagues, yet close enough for me to get back quickly if I'm needed.'

She wondered why he didn't want to run into any of his colleagues but didn't dare ask.

'It's…it's very nice,' she murmured, though in truth she thought the menu ridiculously overpriced and the decor overpowering.

'The food's always excellent,' he observed.

So it should be at these prices, she thought, then groaned inwardly as Gareth began fiddling with his cutlery.

For God's sake, don't just sit here like a dunderhead, her mind urged. The poor man's only asked you out to dinner because you were so upset about Jonah, and now he's probably wondering how quickly he can get rid of you and do something more exciting with his evening like watching paint dry. Say something—say *anything*.

'Gareth—'

'Peggie—'

'You first,' she said hurriedly.

'I was just wondering what made you decide to specialise in plastic surgery, and why plastic surgery for children?'

Well, his question didn't exactly give her an opening for the world's most scintillating conversation, but at least it gave her the opportunity to say something and she grabbed it with both hands.

'It was the six month pre-reg I did in the A and E department of the Belfast General. Sometimes—far too often, in fact—casualties from ''The Troubles'' would come in, and though I felt sorry for the adults it was the children who touched me most. Knowing they faced a lifetime of disfigurement unless somebody helped them.'

'And you decided you wanted to be that somebody?' He smiled.

She nodded. 'What made you decide to specialise in plastic surgery?'

His smile faded. 'It's such a long time ago now, I can't remember, but it was probably for much the same reasons as you. Ah, here's our starter,' he added, reaching for his knife and fork as the waiter arrived carrying two plates of game tureen with Cumberland sauce and Melba toast.

He was lying. She didn't know how she knew it, but she knew he was lying. Whatever his reasons had been for specialising in plastic surgery, they weren't the same as hers.

'I suppose you'll be returning to Ireland once you've gained enough experience at Lizzie's?' he continued before she could say anything.

A slight frown creased her forehead. 'It's something I always planned to do, but now… I'm really enjoying working here, and I've started to make a few friends, and…' She smiled a little uncertainly. 'Now, I'm not certain what my plans are.'

'We'd miss you if you left.'

Her eyes flew to his. We? Did he include himself amongst that 'we'? She'd like to think he did but nothing about his expression gave her a clue as to what he was thinking.

'I expect you'd survive,' she said lightly. 'And I know my replacement would definitely fit the theatre scrubs a whole lot better than I do.'

'Oh, I doubt that very much.'

His eyes were fixed on hers, deep and dark and unfathomable, and she swallowed hard. Was he flirting with her? It certainly sounded very much as though he was flirting with her. Say something witty, clever, her brain urged.

'I think you look very nice in your theatre scrubs too,' she blurted out, then crimsoned when he threw back his head and laughed. 'I'm sorry, I don't know why I said that—'

'Oh, don't apologise,' he declared, his eyes warm, as the waiter cleared away their empty plates and replaced them with noisettes of lamb. 'I think that's quite the nicest compliment anyone's ever paid me.'

'No, it's not, and I'm an idiot for saying it,' she said ruefully. 'The trouble is my tongue always runs away with itself when I'm nervous.'

'I make you nervous?' he said in surprise.

As a cat on a hot tin roof, she thought, forking some lamb into her mouth, but she managed to smile. 'You've got to remember it's not every day a girl gets taken out to dinner by God.'

He groaned. 'Those damn initials of mine—and I've been behaving like a proper so-and-so recently, haven't I?'

She nodded. 'I'm afraid so.'

'I hadn't meant to,' he said softly. 'And if there's one person in the world I wouldn't consciously want to hurt, it's you.'

Her heart gave a sudden flutter against her ribs. This wasn't flirting. She might not be experienced but this wasn't flirting, this was something else.

'Gareth—'

'Did you know your eyes laugh?'

'My eyes do what?' she exclaimed in confusion.

'They laugh. When you're pleased about something, or find something funny—they laugh.'

And there ought to be a law against a man having such

indecently long and curly eyelashes as you do, she wanted to reply, but instead she stammered, 'I-I think you don't laugh enough.'

'Maybe I never had much cause to before,' he murmured.

Did he mean he found her amusing—like a cute, appealing child? She moistened her lips nervously, not wanting to say the wrong thing, and saw something flare in his deep green eyes.

'Gareth—'

'Peggie.'

She'd always hated her name, thought it too old-fashioned, but on his lips it almost sounded like a caress.

'Yes?' she said faintly.

But he didn't say anything. He just reached out and covered her hand gently with his own and suddenly time seemed to hang motionless between them. She didn't see the other diners any more, she didn't even notice the restaurant manager's quizzical glance as he passed them. All she was aware of was the gentle pressure of Gareth's fingers against hers. All she was conscious of was his deep green eyes and her skittering heartbeat.

'Peggie,' he said again, and as he cleared his throat she felt his hand tighten convulsively on hers. 'There's something—'

'Why, *Gary,* what a surprise!'

And one that couldn't possibly have come at a worse time, Peggie thought as Gareth released her hand abruptly and she turned to find herself gazing up into Frances Harper's beautiful face.

'I didn't know this was one of your haunts, Frances,' Gareth observed with a smile that didn't reach his eyes.

'It isn't normally but I'm here with some friends,' she declared, waving airily in the direction of a table somewhere behind her. 'We've been to the theatre and thought we'd just drop into Rosins for a meal. Perhaps you and your SHO—Meggie, isn't it?—would like to join us?'

'I'm sorry but *Peggie* and I are just leaving,' he declared, motioning quickly to the hovering waiter.

'But you haven't finished your meal,' the physiotherapist protested.

'I don't think either of us are very hungry any more, Frances,' he said dryly.

And she most certainly wasn't, Peggie decided as Gareth all but bundled her out of the restaurant and into his car. In fact just the thought of having Frances Harper's blue eyes fixed inquisitively on her for the rest of the meal was enough to completely take away her appetite.

'I shouldn't have dragged you away from Rosins like that,' Gareth said when he drew his car to a halt outside the hospital flats. 'It was neither polite nor gracious of me, and I apologise.'

'There's no need to,' she insisted. 'Frances...Frances isn't exactly my favourite person either.'

He smiled but said nothing, and an awkward silence descended on the car.

Say something even if it's something stupid, her mind urged. If you don't, he'll simply say goodnight, and drive away, and you know you don't want the evening to end, not yet.

She took a deep breath and her courage in her hands. 'Do you...would you like to come up to my flat for some coffee?'

For a moment she thought—hoped—he was going to say yes, then he shook his head. 'I'd better not. It's late.'

Late? Not even in Leoanen was half-past ten considered late.

Can't you take a hint? her mind whispered. He wants rid of you, so just thank him nicely for the evening, and get out of the car.

'I'll say goodnight, then,' she said awkwardly, reaching for her bag. 'And...and thank you for the meal. It was very kind of you.'

'I'm glad you enjoyed it.'

It sounded like a dismissal—it certainly felt like one, she thought unhappily, and quickly fumbled for the car door handle.

'Let me help,' Gareth declared, stretching across her.

Lord, but he really must want rid of her, she thought, shaking her head. 'I've got it, thank you—'

'You haven't—you're turning it the wrong way—'

'I can manage—'

And she probably would have if she hadn't somehow ended up entangled in his arms as they each tried to open the car door at the same time.

For an instant she froze, willing herself not to react to the feel of his muscular arms around her, fully expecting him to release her immediately, but he didn't. Instead he stared deep into her eyes, then suddenly reached up and cupped her face in his hands.

Was he going to kiss her this time? she wondered, her heart-rate going into overdrive. Was he going to kiss her, or would it be the same as last time and she'd spend days wondering?

'Gareth—'

She didn't get a chance to say anything else. His lips came down on hers, capturing them, and her heart bucked against her chest.

In her dreams his kiss had always been gentle but there was nothing gentle about the lips that claimed hers. His mouth was hungry, seeking and demanding, and there was nothing she could do—nothing she wanted to do—but surrender to that hunger and meet it with a passion of her own.

Even when he slid his hand up inside her sweater and cupped her breast with his firm, lean fingers all she wanted was for him to continue touching her. When he freed her breasts from her bra and caressed first one and then the other into aching, throbbing points of delight with his mouth all she wanted was to have him closer, closer.

Somewhere in the deep recesses of her mind she realised there was something faintly ridiculous about a woman of her age losing her virginity in a car, but when she locked her arms around his neck to bring him nearer and felt the patent evidence of his own arousal she ceased to think at all.

All she knew was that she wanted this man and the result would have been a foregone conclusion if a sudden burst of laughter from a crowd of nurses passing hadn't caused him to release her abruptly.

'It's all right, they've gone,' she said breathlessly, watching the nurses until they disappeared into the flats.

He didn't say a word and she turned to him with concern. 'Gareth, what is it—what's wrong?'

'Peggie, I'm sorry,' he said unsteadily, his breathing ragged. 'So sorry.'

'For what?' she said in confusion. 'Gareth—'

'I made a mistake,' he interrupted, his face curiously haggard under the lamplight. 'An unforgivable one. Now, please—while I still have some remnants of control left—get out of the car.'

'Get out of the car?' she repeated, staring at him bewildered.

'Believe me, it's for the best,' he declared, his voice tight. 'I should never have kissed you—I never intended to kiss you.'

'You're sorry you kissed me?' she echoed faintly. 'You never intended to kiss me?'

'Peggie…' He paused and bit his lip. 'I know I owe you some sort of explanation but right now… Please…will you just get out of the car?'

And she did, though her legs were trembling so much she could barely stand.

'Gareth—'

'Not now, Peggie, OK?' he said hoarsely. 'Later…later.'

And without another word he pulled the passenger door shut, switched on his ignition, slammed his car into gear, and drove away leaving her gazing unhappily after him.

Chapter Six

'As you can see from the X-rays, Esther was born with both a classic cleft lip and palate,' Gareth observed.

'The condition's actually becoming more common, isn't it?' Peggie murmured as she stared at the plates.

'It is. One in seven hundred babies according to the last statistical report and of every nine affected babies, two have a cleft lip, three have a cleft palate, and four have both.'

'And though one third of babies have a relative with one or more deformities,' Peggie said, stepping back from the display screen so Bob Bremen could get a better look at the X-rays, 'that still leaves a staggering two thirds who don't.'

A faint smile appeared on Gareth's face. 'You've clearly been reading up on the subject.'

'I like to be prepared,' was all she replied as she snapped on her surgical gloves and pulled up her mask.

'The condition is caused by the failure of certain clefts in the region of the throat and face to unite, isn't it?' Bob observed, glancing hesitantly from Gareth to Peggie, and back again.

For a second Gareth's gaze remained on Peggie, his expression unreadable, then he nodded. 'The clefts which form part of our noses, the central part of the upper lip, and the upper jaw and palate, should unite completely prior to birth, but if they don't a Y-shaped gap is left and depending on the severity of the gap the child will be born with either a cleft lip, or palate, or both.'

'And is it always better to operate on a cleft lip when the child is very young?' Bob asked, as Gareth switched off the display screen and led the way into the operating theatre.

'Most definitely. The operation isn't a difficult one, and, as it enables the child to feed more easily afterwards, I prefer to do it as soon as possible after birth. Correcting a cleft palate, on the other hand, is a much bigger operation which is why I've chosen to wait until Esther is eighteen months old. Now, if there are no more questions,' he continued, his gaze lingering for a moment on Peggie, 'let's get to work. Everything OK your end, Jack?'

'Fine, boss.'

'Sally?'

'No problems here, Gareth.'

'What about you, Peggie?'

She nodded, and felt her heart twist inside her when she saw the unmistakable look of relief in his eyes.

He'd been avoiding her. Ever since that night three weeks ago when he'd taken her to Rosins and kissed her, he'd been avoiding her.

He'd done it subtly, of course. A changed theatre roster here, an altered lunch break there, but only an idiot would have failed to realise he'd been doing his level best to ensure they saw as little of each other as possible.

Face it, Peggie, her mind whispered as he began the painstaking work of pairing the edges of Esther's open palate prior to drawing the soft parts together across it. You might have found his kiss wonderful, but he clearly didn't so it's about time you forgot all about it and got on with your life.

And she had been trying to. Every morning when she got up she vowed that today she would be able to look him in the eyes and feel nothing. And every day when his shuttered eyes fell on her, her heart died just a little bit more inside her.

How could she have so badly misread the signals he had seemed to be sending out to her? She might be inexperienced but everything about the way he'd behaved, the things he'd said, and even that kiss, had suggested he was every bit as attracted to her as she was to him.

If only she could talk to somebody about it—ask their advice. Sally, for example, would undoubtedly have been able to put her straight, but right now the staff nurse clearly had troubles of her own if her chalk-white face was anything to go by.

'Vital signs, Jack?' Gareth murmured as he began pairing the edges of Esther's palate.

'Pulse 110, respiration normal, heartbeat 110 over 70.'

The anaesthetist sounded abstracted, preoccupied, and Gareth glanced across at him sharply. 'Something wrong, Jack?'

'Not a thing, boss,' he replied with an unconvincing smile.

Something was most definitely wrong, Peggie thought as Gareth returned to his work and Jack stared across at Sally, his brown eyes troubled.

The anaesthetist had seemed so happy since Sally had agreed to go out with him, and Sally… Sally couldn't have been happier if she'd won the lottery and yet today she looked as though her whole world had suddenly collapsed.

'What sort of sutures do you use in an operation like this?' Bob asked as Gareth began pulling the soft parts of Esther's palate together over the gap.

'Absorbable catgut so they don't have to be removed later. What—no comment, Peggie?' he added, his eyebrows rising quizzically as he reached for his forceps.

'Should I have?' she asked.

'I'd have thought this was the moment when you told me the reaction to buried catgut is generally considered to be greater than to synthetic materials like Vicryl?'

She knew he was smiling at her from behind his mask but she didn't smile back.

'I wouldn't presume to tell you anything, Gareth,' she said evenly.

A flash of anger appeared in his deep green eyes for an instant, then he turned to Bob Bremen.

'The reaction to buried catgut can be greater than to synthetics like Vicryl and Dexon,' he declared, his voice tight, 'but a lot depends on the volume of the buried material. If you use 6-0 catgut there is very little tissue reaction.'

What did he expect from her? she wondered as he began suturing Esther's palate, his face an implacable mask. That she could pretend nothing had happened? That she could look at him and not remember that kiss?

He expects you to be mature and sensible about it, her mind replied. He expects you to regard that kiss as lightly and dismissively as he does.

Well, she didn't feel mature and sensible, she thought angrily. She might be twenty-five soon but she still felt hurt, and let down, and used, and if that made her immature, she was immature.

'The operation you've just performed on Esther,' Bob observed when Esther had been carefully wheeled through into Recovery. 'Will it be the only one she'll require?'

'I'm hoping so,' Gareth replied. 'Sometimes further operations are needed, but if we're lucky dental management and speech therapy will be all she needs.'

Luck had nothing to do with it, Peggie thought as she went quickly through to the changing room and put on a fresh set of theatre scrubs in preparation for the next operation. With Gareth's deft hands using the scalpel the little girl's troubles were undoubtedly over. She just wished her own troubles could be solved quite so readily.

And Sally's too, she decided as the girl came into the changing room and stood abstractedly at one of the sinks.

'Don't say it,' Sally said quickly, looking round and seeing Peggie's worried gaze on her. 'I can tell from the look on your face you're itching to give me some more of that claptrap about a trouble shared being a trouble halved, and I don't want to hear it, OK?'

'OK,' Peggie murmured uncertainly.

Swiftly Sally pulled off her cap but before she could bin it a muffled sob came from her.

'Sally—'

'He's dumped me, Peggie. Last night—when Jack took me back to my flat after we'd been out to dinner—he said he thought it might be better if we didn't see each other any more.'

'Oh, Sally—'

'He said getting involved with someone you worked with led to all sorts of complications,' the girl continued, her bottom lip trembling. 'Then he said I was a really nice girl, a very special girl, and a lot more of the same rubbish, but I knew the bottom line was that he was dumping me like he's done every other girl who's been stupid enough to go out with him.'

'Oh, Sally, I'm so sorry,' Peggie declared, her heart going out to her. 'Look, maybe if I talked to him—'

'Don't you dare,' the staff nurse gasped. 'Have him think I asked you to? No way—never!'

'Sally—'

'I've still got my pride,' the girl continued, dashing a hand across her eyes. 'I might not have anything else left right now, but I've still got that!'

'But—'

Peggie didn't get a chance to finish what she'd been about to say. As Gareth swung into the changing room Sally took one look at him and with a smothered cry dashed into one of the cubicles.

'What on earth's going on in here?' he demanded. 'What's happened?'

'Sally's a bit upset about something, that's all,' Peggie said awkwardly. 'It's nothing that need concern you.'

'It does concern me if it's something which might affect her efficiency in the theatre,' he replied with a deep frown.

'It won't,' she said firmly. 'Sally's a professional. We're all professionals. Nothing—*nothing,*' she repeated, meeting and holding his gaze, 'affects our work.'

It was he who looked away first, and his voice when he spoke was low. 'Peggie, we need to talk.'

'I thought that's what we were doing?' she replied, deliberately cool, though her heart had started to beat in an erratic fashion.

'You know what I mean,' he murmured. 'I promised you an explanation, and it's long overdue.'

It was, but suddenly she wasn't at all sure she wanted to hear it.

'I'm pretty tied up today, Gareth,' she said quickly. 'Tomorrow's not a whole lot better, and Friday—'

'Charlotte Heath's arrived, Peggie,' Jack announced, swinging open the changing-room door. 'She's already had her premed so do you want me to put her under?'

'Please.' She nodded, hoping Gareth would simply let the matter drop but he didn't.

'What about lunch time?' he said as soon as the door of the changing room had clattered shut.

Something about his face told her she most definitely wouldn't want to hear what he had to say and she shook her head. 'I have plans for lunch.'

'After work, then?' he pressed. 'I should be finished by seven.'

'I'm on emergency stand-by tonight.'

'Peggie—'

'Did Jack just say Charlotte Heath had arrived?' Sally asked, emerging suddenly from her cubicle.

Peggie nodded.

'So are we going to operate on her, or stand about here talking all day?' the girl demanded.

Peggie gazed at Sally searchingly. The girl's eyes might

be a little red, her face a bit blotchy, but other than that she looked in control again.

'We're going to operate,' she said with a smile.

Chicken, she told herself as she led the way into the operating theatre, deliberately avoiding Gareth's gaze. If you talk to the man he can tell you why he behaved the way he did that night, and you can tell him…

What? she demanded, selecting a scalpel. That his kiss made you feel like you've never felt before, and you want more of the same, please? No, I don't think so.

But don't you want to know why he apologised for kissing you, why he's been avoiding you? her heart asked.

Yes, she wanted to know, but the trouble was that she knew with absolute certainty that she wasn't going to like the answer.

'Try to cut as conservatively as you can,' Gareth observed as she began removing the sections of skin where the dirt had become tattooed into Charlotte's face. 'We want to remove as much of the damaged skin as possible, but don't forget you're going to be creating other scars and we want them to be as small as possible.'

She nodded. Both she and Gareth had already explained to Charlotte's parents that there was no miracle cure for their daughter's disfigurement, but Mr and Mrs Heath had decided they wanted the operation carried out and Peggie was determined to perform it to the best of her abilities.

'If you insert a skin hook at the end of each wound and insert a few key sutures first, that should keep the skin taut,' he commented after she had cut out all the tattooed dirt and selected as more appropriate a pair of toothed dissecting forceps and a needle. 'It's all too easy when you're performing surgery like this for the skin to sag.'

'Would you prefer to carry out the operation yourself?' she asked, trying and failing to keep the edge out of her voice.

His eyes caught hers. 'You wouldn't be doing it at all if I didn't have complete faith in your ability.'

She bit her lip behind her mask. He was only trying to help, she knew he was, but right now she'd have preferred him to be on the far side of the moon.

And it didn't get any easier when she had finished the operation. She accompanied Jack into the recovery room to watch him give the little girl an antidote to the anaesthetic in order to wake her up and Gareth followed them there. She went swiftly into one of the changing cubicles and was deliberately slow in getting into her blouse and skirt but when she finally emerged it was to find him waiting.

Nothing, it seemed, was going to dissuade him from his attempt to talk to her and she had just resigned herself to the inevitable when to her relief his bleeper sounded.

'Later, OK, Peggie?' he said as he went out the door. 'We'll talk later.'

Later was a whole lot better than now, she thought. Later she might be calmer, less angry, less emotional.

Fat chance, Peggie, her heart whispered as she left the changing room. Fat chance.

There was one situation she had no intention of running away from, however, she decided as she saw Jack walking along the corridor ahead of her. Sally might have said she wasn't to interfere but the girl was her friend and she hated seeing her so unhappy.

Quickly she hastened her step and soon caught up with him.

'Hi, Peggie.' He smiled. 'Are you on your way back to the unit or going for lunch? If it's lunch, I know this quiet little bistro near the hospital—'

'Jack, I know it's none of my business,' she interrupted, 'but Sally's very upset.'

To her surprise his blond eyebrows snapped down. 'You're right—it is none of your business.'

'Jack, I know you like her—and she really likes you,'

she persevered. 'If there's a problem surely you can work it out?'

'A problem—oh, yeah, there's a problem,' he declared, his handsome face suddenly bitter. 'And it's not one you can fix with any of your scalpels, Dr O'Neill.'

'Jack—'

'Peggie, sometimes relationships work out, sometimes they don't, and it's better to cut your losses before someone gets really hurt.'

'I think you're both already hurt,' she observed. 'I think you're in love with Sally and for some stupid reason you just don't want to admit it.'

'And I think it's high time you stopped playing match-maker, Peggie, and got your own damn private life sorted out!' he snapped, and before she could say anything he whirled on his heel, leaving her gazing open-mouthed after him.

Well, that'll teach you to interfere in someone else's love life, she told herself as she walked down to the canteen and picked up a sandwich. That'll teach you to poke your nose in where it's clearly not wanted.

And what in the world ever made you think you could give Jack advice anyway? her thoughts persisted as she left the hospital and made her way to Regent's Park. It's your birthday next week and all you've got to show for your twenty-five years of living is a string of medical qualifications and a big fat zero in the personal relationship stakes.

A wry chuckle broke from her as she sat down on her old bench and began eating her sandwich. She should have been asking Jack's advice, not trying to give him some.

'I hope that's not all you're eating today?'

Her heart sank to the foot of her stomach as she looked up and saw Gareth staring down at her, his green eyes suspicious.

'I had a huge breakfast, and I'll be having dinner in the canteen tonight,' she replied. 'I just wanted to get some fresh air and bringing a sandwich to the park seemed the best way to do it.'

Not to mention the fact that I'd hoped there would be less chance of running into you out here, she added inwardly.

'May I join you?' he asked.

Last time he hadn't asked, she remembered as she slid along the bench to make room for him. Last time he had just sat down.

'I thought Esther Black's operation went very well this morning,' he observed.

Oh, Lord. They were going to talk about work, the last resort of the desperate or the terminally bored—and she didn't think he was bored.

'It will make a huge difference to her,' she said, throwing the remnants of her sandwich to the waiting ducks. 'She'll start putting on weight now and with speech therapy her voice should become quite normal.'

'You approve of surgery in Esther's case, then?' he said, leaning back against the bench to gaze at her.

'Of course I do,' she exclaimed, knowing full well he was referring to Liam Docherty who was due to have his first operation to alter his appearance in July. 'Esther's condition affects her eating and growth. What I'm not happy about is performing surgery simply to make a child more acceptable to society. We should be persuading that society to look for the real loving person underneath the purely visual disfigurement.'

'If you think we'll ever be able to do that, Peggie, then you have a very optimistic opinion of humanity,' he said dryly. 'Everybody—except perhaps for very young children—judges by outward appearance.'

She rolled up her paper bag and threw it into the litter bin. 'And you, I think, have a very jaundiced view of the human race.'

She thought he was going to argue with her—he certainly looked as though he was about to—then clearly changed his mind.

'Peggie, I owe you an explanation for my behaviour after I took you to Rosins that night. When I kissed you—and I know I should never have kissed you,' he continued quickly as she tried to interrupt, 'my actions might have implied— might have suggested—that something could develop out of our relationship.'

'And you're saying it can't,' she said with a calmness she was very far from feeling.

He nodded. 'Peggie, you're a very attractive girl, a very special girl.'

'But?'

'I'm sorry?' he said in confusion.

'I hear a "but" in that,' she said. 'I'm a very attractive girl, a very special girl, but…?'

'Relationships…relationships between people who work together—they so often start simply because the people concerned are constantly being thrown together. Feelings become distorted, emotions confused, and when reality finally creeps in… It can be devastating for the people concerned.'

It sounded so much like a carbon copy of what Jack had said to Sally that she almost laughed in his face. Almost but not quite. Right now she was too angry, too hurt, to see the irony of the situation.

'Tom and his wife seem very happy, and he met her when she was working at Lizzie's,' she said tightly.

'Jane didn't work in Plastics, she worked in Radiology.'

'What about Amanda Grayson and Edward Burrows in Out-patients, or Lyn Webster and Ross McKinnon in Neurology—?'

'OK, OK, there are always exceptions,' he interrupted.

'Why don't you just tell the truth?' she demanded. 'That you don't want to be seen going out with a walking disaster area?'

'A walking—'

'That's what I heard you tell Tom.'

A deep tide of colour darkened his cheeks. 'You weren't supposed to hear that,' he said uncomfortably, 'and I was wrong—totally wrong—and I can only apologise.'

She didn't want his apology—she didn't want any more of his apologies—she wanted answers.

'Look, I know I'm too small,' she began. 'And I know I'm definitely too fat—'

'You're not fat,' he protested. 'You look exactly as a woman is supposed to look, not like some walking coat-hanger.'

Then what's wrong with me? she wanted to cry. Why flirt with me, why kiss me as you did, if you're not attracted to me?

And he hadn't explained anything, she realised. He'd said he shouldn't have kissed her. He'd said he might have inadvertently given her the wrong idea. What he hadn't explained was why he'd kissed her in the first place.

'Gareth—'

The shrill sound of his bleeper rent the air and he got to his feet immediately. 'I have to go.'

She could stay in Regent's Park and brood, or...

'I'm coming with you.'

'There's probably no need—'

'Then I'll have got some exercise for nothing,' she interrupted firmly, and a wry smile curved his lips as they began to run towards the hospital.

'There was no need to break the speed limit, Gareth.' Daniel Burr, A and E's specialist registrar, grinned when he saw them.

'It's good for the image, Daniel.' Gareth smiled. 'What's the situation?'

'Pretty confused. A ten-year-old boy called Steven Yu was brought in by his grandparents half an hour ago and from the few words of English they can speak we think

Steven got his hand trapped in the hot press in their laundry.'

'Where are the boy's parents?' Gareth asked.

'As far as I can make out they're on their way to a wedding in Newcastle which is why I've sent for David Chang. With luck he might be able to translate for us. Ah,' he added with relief as the nurse came through the door. 'The very man we need.'

But when Daniel had explained the situation David Chang shook his head ruefully. 'Sorry. My parents might have come from Hong Kong originally but I'm afraid I don't speak a word of Chinese.'

'Well, that stymies that idea,' Gareth exclaimed. 'OK, let's take a look at the boy.'

His examination didn't tell them any more than Daniel Burr had. It was quite obvious the hand was badly burned but Steven was almost unconscious with pain and his grandparents could only weep and shake their heads in bewilderment to any question put to them.

'The only thing we can do is get him up to the theatre and take a proper look,' Gareth said eventually. 'The hand looks relatively normal apart from being very badly burnt but until I operate I really can't tell what we're going to find. It could need some simple skin grafts—I've a feeling it could need a whole lot more. Daniel, could you get the grandparents to sign a general consent form, and we'll take it from there?'

Within minutes all the necessary paperwork had been completed and not only had Steven arrived at the operating theatre but Peggie and Gareth and Tom were scrubbed up and ready to go.

'Does anyone have any idea how hot something like a laundry press can get?' Gareth asked as he made his first incision into the young boy's hand.

'About two hundred and ten degrees centigrade,' Jack replied, and coloured slightly as everyone looked across at him in surprise. 'I used to work in a laundry at the weekend to make extra cash when I was a student,' he explained. 'And as ironing other people's clothes wasn't exactly the most riveting of jobs, I got interested in the machine side of the business.'

'Two hundred and ten degrees centigrade,' Gareth echoed. 'Something tells me we're not going to be looking at just a few skin grafts here.'

He was right. When he peeled back the badly burned skin on Steven's hand Tom let out a gasp of horror.

'Bloody hell, Gareth, the whole middle part of his hand has been cooked!'

It had, and there was clearly no chance whatsoever of it surviving. And with no connection to the body's blood supply, Steven's fingers were also effectively dead.

'I'm afraid it looks like an amputation job.' Tom sighed.

Gareth frowned for a moment, then shook his head. 'I think we can save the hand. I think we can resuscitate and preserve the fingers.'

Tom looked at him dubiously. 'We could certainly try taking out the middle of his hand and transplanting the fingers back on, taking nerve and tendon grafts from other parts of his body—'

'Which is still going to leave him with a very badly deformed and virtually useless right hand,' Gareth interrupted.

'So what's your idea?' Peggie asked.

'I think three of his fingers are salvageable,' he replied. 'And I think I could preserve them by joining them to an artery in his left arm. We could leave the fingers there until I can begin reconstructing his hand and transplant them back later.'

'But you'd have to leave his fingers joined to the artery in his arm for at least eight months,' Peggie said uncertainly. 'Will he be up to it—psychologically, I mean? He's only ten. How's he going to feel when he wakes up to find that he's not only lost his hand but the fingers of the amputated hand are attached to his left arm?'

'And we'd have to join the stump of his hand to his groin for the resurfacing of the burnt skin,' Tom observed. 'It's a hell of a thing to expect a ten-year-old to cope with, Gareth.'

'It's that or have no useful right hand at all,' he replied. 'And hands are like faces—they're something people always notice. So, do I do it or not?' he continued.

For a second the specialist registrar chewed his lower lip, then nodded. 'If you think you can pull it off, go for it.'

'Peggie?' Gareth asked, turning to her.

'How long will it take before you can give Steven a useful working hand again?'

'Four—maybe five years. Reconstructive surgery takes a long time, Peggie.'

'But you can give him a working hand eventually?'

He nodded. 'I think so.'

'Then do it,' she said.

And he did.

The operation was a long and gruelling one, and by the time it was finished the whole team was exhausted.

'Are you OK, Tom?' Peggie asked as Gareth accompanied Jack and Sally through to the recovery room and she noticed the specialist registrar rubbing his hands wearily across his face.

'It's nothing a good night's sleep wouldn't cure.' He smiled ruefully. 'I love my daughter dearly, Peggie, but I have to confess there are times when I wish I could fit a silencer to her. If it's not "Daddy, do this," it's "Daddy, come and see this," and when you're trying to study for your MRCS exams...' He shook his head. 'Sometimes I think Gareth has the right idea—no family, no commitments, no distractions.'

'Do you really think so?' she said a little wistfully, and he sighed.

'Don't go falling for him, love.'

'I'm not,' she protested.

'Peggie, you're a nice girl, a sweet girl, and the last thing I want is to see you being hurt.'

'And you think I would be?' she murmured.

'I *know* you could be,' he said firmly. 'Peggie, I've worked for Gareth for three years—I'm the closest to a friend he's got at Lizzie's—and yet I've never been invited to his house. Relationships—even friendships—don't seem important to him.'

'But—'

'Some blokes are just made that way, love. Their career is everything to them and there's no room in their lives for anything or anyone else. Please, don't go falling for him. You'll only end up being very badly hurt.'

Jack had warned her not to fall in love with Gareth, she remembered, and now Tom was doing it too. The trouble was it was too late for warnings. She'd already lost her heart. Lost it to a man who didn't want it, and who was probably never going to want it.

Wearily she changed out of her theatre pyjamas and walked pensively to the plastic surgery unit. If she was lucky she might get a quiet night on emergency stand-by. If she was even luckier she might actually be able to get on with some studying provided a pair of deep green eyes didn't keep coming creeping unbidden into her mind.

By sheer will-power she kept her attention on her books but a phone call from A and E just after midnight to say that three children who'd been trapped in a house fire were expected in half an hour had her immediately dialling Gareth's home number.

There was no way she could deal with the situation on her own. She needed help, and she needed it fast, but the phone continued to ring and ring for an eternity and she was just on the point of giving up and phoning Tom when the receiver was finally lifted.

'Gareth, it's Peggie,' she declared without preamble. 'We've got an emergency on the way—'

'And I'm not Gareth, I'm afraid,' a soft feminine voice interrupted with a chuckle.

For a moment Peggie stared blankly at the phone, then pulled herself together. Of course he would have a live-in housekeeper. He was a senior consultant. He probably needed one for entertaining, for business lunches, for…for…

'Are you still there?' the disembodied voice asked a little uncertainly.

'Yes, yes, I'm still here,' Peggie replied quickly. 'Could you tell Mr Davies that Peggie O'Neill phoned to say he's needed back at the hospital right away?'

'Wouldn't you rather speak to him yourself?' the soft voice suggested. 'He's bound to want to know what the emergency is and there's no point in telling me—I'll probably get it all wrong.'

'If you're sure it's not too much trouble?' Peggie said.

'Of course it's not any trouble,' the woman replied. 'We weren't in bed yet anyway.'

Weren't in bed yet? Peggie shook her head vexedly. Of course the woman didn't mean they normally went to bed together. It was just an expression, a figure of speech; it didn't mean anything.

'That would be very kind of you,' she murmured.

'Not at all,' the soft female voice reassured her.

She must have put the phone down because the next thing Peggie heard was her voice calling, 'Gareth—darling—it's someone for you from the hospital.' And then the equally clear sound of him calling back, 'I'll be there in a minute, sweetheart.'

And as she waited for him to come to the phone one thought reverberated round and round Peggie's brain.

He was married. Gareth Davies was married.

Chapter Seven

HAPPY birthday, Peggie, she thought as she stared down from her consulting-room window at the colourful tulips in the flower tubs outside the hospital. You're twenty-five-years old today, in love for the very first time, and the man's married.

But he can't be married, her heart protested as it had done ever since she'd made that fateful phone call to Gareth's home six days ago. How could he have kept a wife hidden from everyone at Lizzie's for the last three years? Where the hell had she been—locked in a cupboard?

She wouldn't need to be locked in a cupboard, she realised. Gareth never attends any hospital functions, he never invites anyone back to his home, and he'd told you himself he ate at Rosins because none of his colleagues did.

But what kind of wife would be prepared to live like that? What kind of wife never phoned her husband at work, or left messages for him to pick up some milk or the dry cleaning on his way home?

Maybe he wasn't married. Maybe he had a live-in girlfriend who was chronically shy. But then why keep it a secret? And why, when he'd told her their relationship could never develop into anything, hadn't he simply said he was in a long-term relationship he didn't want to end? She would have accepted it. She wouldn't have liked it. She would have felt deceived and used, but she would have accepted it.

'Peggie, you're not forgetting we're due in theatre in forty minutes to help Tom with Graeme Wright's hypospadias op, are you?' Sally said as she opened the consulting-room door.

'I hadn't forgotten,' she murmured.

The girl looked at her uncertainly for a moment, then came in and closed the door. 'Peggie, are you OK?'

'Not exactly,' she replied with a watery smile, 'but I expect I'll survive.'

The staff nurse shook her head and sighed. 'You've got man trouble, haven't you?'

'I didn't think it was that obvious,' Peggie exclaimed ruefully, and Sally chuckled.

'Only to a fellow sufferer. It's Gareth, isn't it?'

'Sally—'

'I'm not going to dash out and spread it around the hospital, if that's what you're thinking,' she protested, seeing Peggie's panic-stricken expression. 'I've got problems of my own, remember, what with half of Lizzie's feeling sorry for me, and the other half thinking I'm a fool to have got myself into this situation in the first place.'

'Isn't there any chance of you and Jack getting back together again?' Peggie asked.

Sally shook her head. 'As far as Jack's concerned I'm history—just one more entry in his little black book.'

'And you—how do you feel?'

Tears brimmed for a second in the staff nurse's eyes and she blinked them away rapidly. 'I'm still stuck on the guy. Pathetic, isn't it?'

'If you're pathetic, I'm afraid I must be too.' Peggie sighed.

'No hope for you, then, either?'

'Nope,' Peggie replied, forcing a smile to her lips.

'I tell you what,' Sally observed. 'Why don't we both just accept that all men are rat finks, and adopt a policy of celibacy from now on?'

Because I don't want to be celibate, Peggie thought unhappily. I want to be wrapped in Gareth Davies' arms, losing my damn virginity, that's what I want.

'Boy, you've really got it bad, haven't you?' Sally declared, watching her. 'Look, maybe I can help. If you tell me what the problem is, perhaps I can come up with a solution.'

'For a man who's just not interested?' Peggie said sadly.

'But he is interested,' Sally protested. 'Lord, if ever a man was stuck on someone, it's Gareth on you.' She frowned. 'Unless he's just been playing silly games, and I wouldn't have thought he was the type.'

Neither would I, Peggie thought, but the more she considered it, the more she wondered if perhaps Sally hadn't come up with the right answer, and a surge of anger flooded through her.

Had he simply been amusing himself at her expense? Had he thought it might be fun to string her along and see how far she'd go? Well, if that was his game, the game was over. She wasn't going to play any more.

'What are you thinking?' Sally asked curiously as a small smile crept across Peggie's face.

'About something my mother used to say back home in Ireland,' she murmured. 'Don't get mad—get even.'

The staff nurse's jaw dropped, then her eyes sparkled. 'What are you going to do?'

'I don't know,' Peggie admitted, leading the way out of her consulting room, 'but I'll think of something, believe me.'

'You might be able to come up with something a whole lot sooner than you think,' Sally observed. 'Bob Bremen's put in for a transfer.'

Peggie halted. 'You're joking?'

Sally shook her head. 'He saw Gareth yesterday and told him he was sorry but he just wasn't happy in Plastics.'

'But where will he go? It isn't easy getting a transfer, and—'

'Lucas Morrison's offered him a post in Orthopaedics. Apparently Bob's been spending every spare minute of his time down there, and Lucas is really impressed.'

Peggie had been too, but she'd thought the junior doctor was simply interested in Paul Marshall's skin-flap operation, not that he was considering changing specialisations.

'Which means that July is going to be a real fun month for us with Angel leaving then, too,' Sally continued. 'It will be absolute chaos until we get used to working with two new people.'

Just an hour ago Peggie might have been tempted to say the team would have to get used to working with three new people, but not now.

Why the hell should she leave? she decided as she and Sally made their way to the operating theatre. She had a job she enjoyed, doing work she loved, and if her presence made Gareth uncomfortable—and it very plainly did—then tough.

It was time she stopped behaving like a wimp. It was time she grew up and discovered there were plenty more fish in the sea. And if they weren't like Gareth Davies, then so much the better.

'I was beginning to think you'd forgotten all about me.' Tom grinned when they arrived.

'As if.' Sally chuckled. 'Is Graeme ready?'

'He's had his premed so whenever you're both scrubbed up Jack can put him under.'

'This hypospadias Graeme suffers from—it's a congenital defect of the penis, isn't it?' Peggie observed as Sally disappeared into one of the changing cubicles.

Tom nodded. 'It affects around one in three hundred male babies. The opening of the urethra is situated on the underside of the penis instead of at the tip, and in some cases the penis curves downwards—a condition known as chordee—and the foreskin is limited to the front of the penis.'

'And you're going to straighten out the penis and use a tube of skin to create a new urethra?'

'Got it in one,' Tom replied.

It wasn't a long operation. Luckily Graeme's parents hadn't had him circumcised so there was enough foreskin to cover the whole of the penis and within an hour the toddler was back in Recovery.

Peggie's hopes of grabbing an early lunch were dashed, however, when Tom revealed that Gareth was expecting her down in IC to help him take skin grafts from the boy who was badly burned in the house fire last week.

'But I thought you were going to assist?' she protested.

'So did I, but Gareth felt you might like the practice.'

She would, but as she went down to IC it was anger she felt, not gratitude.

Ever since he'd told her last week that relationships between people who worked together seldom worked out Gareth had been tiptoeing round her as though she were an invalid in need of special care. Every time she looked up she found his gaze on her. Every time she turned round he was there, hovering. He was clearly feeling guilty, and his way of dealing with it was to fall over himself to be nice to her.

Well, if what Sally had said about him playing games was true, he sure as hell ought to feel guilty. Stringing her along like that, making her feel special, kissing her... Dammit, if those nurses hadn't appeared when they had he would have made love to her, and she would have let him.

Well, enough, Peggie, she thought, hardening her heart as she saw him waiting for her outside IC. She might be naive but she wasn't a fool.

'Any problems upstairs with Graeme Wright's op?' he asked as she joined him.

For a second she was tempted to say yes, there had been. For an even longer second she was tempted to say they'd been raided by the drugs squad halfway through the operation and they'd only released her when she'd told them her boss was an absolute louse, but she resisted the impulse.

'Everything went fine,' she replied evenly.

In fact, a lot better and less stressful than returning to IC always was, she thought, unconsciously taking a deep breath as he opened the door of IC and stood back to let her go in ahead of him.

She still found it difficult coming in here even though it was weeks since Jonah had died. No matter how hard she tried, she couldn't stop her eyes drifting to the bed he'd occupied and part of her still half expected to see his smiling brown eyes gazing back at her.

'Look, would you rather not assist me?' Gareth asked, understanding plain in his voice. 'I could phone Tom—'

'There's no need,' she interrupted. 'I'm fine.'

'You don't look fine,' he observed gently. 'You look pale and tired and stressed.'

She clenched her hands together tightly. She didn't want his concern—a concern born out of guilt. She just wanted him to start treating her like one of the team again and then maybe—maybe—she would get over him.

'I'm fine,' she repeated through clenched teeth, and he sighed as she swung past him and into the ward.

She wasn't fine. He knew perfectly well she wasn't fine but he'd done the right thing, he told himself, watching her exchange a laughing word with Sister Gilbert. He'd backed off before either of them got hurt. He'd done the right thing so he should have felt noble and good, and instead he felt lousy. Lousy, and frustrated, and a louse.

She didn't smile at him any more. Her eyes didn't light up when she saw him and she was all too plainly uncomfortable in his presence. What did you expect? he asked himself. You should have told her the truth—she would have understood.

Oh, yeah, he thought bitterly, like Marianne and Julia had understood? Marianne who'd been his SHO at the Swansea Infirmary, and yet after two years of living with him hadn't been able to bear it any more. And Julia who had said it didn't matter but who couldn't ever bear to see the reality.

It was better this way, he reminded himself, and if that better felt hellish right now, the feeling would pass. Everything passed in time.

'Hi, Gareth, Peggie—come to see our celebrity patient, have you?' Sam Harrison observed, his eyes twinkling as he walked down the ward towards them.

'He certainly is a celebrity, isn't he?' Peggie smiled back. 'And quite right too. If it hadn't been for his prompt and very brave actions his little brother and sister would be lying beside him now in IC instead of being released so quickly with just smoke inhalation.'

'I'm afraid poor Steven Yu's nose has been put quite out of joint by it all.' Sam laughed. 'He was kingpin of IC before, but with Christopher's face splashed all over the newspapers he's having to take a back seat, and he doesn't like it one bit.'

'So I've just heard from Sister Gilbert.' Peggie chuckled.

Far from being harmed psychologically by the operation on his hand as she and Tom had feared, young Steven positively revelled in the unorthodox position of his fingers and had, in fact, to be constantly dissuaded from showing them to anyone and everyone who came into the ward.

It looked unlikely they were going to have the same problem with Christopher. Far from showing any desire to display the spectacular burns on his arms and legs, Christopher looked as though he wished himself a million miles away as Sister Gilbert pulled the screens round his bed.

'This really isn't going to hurt, Christopher,' Peggie said reassuringly as the boy stared up at her, fear and pain clear in his eyes. 'In fact, you might actually find it interesting.'

'I doubt it,' the boy murmured. 'I mean, do you know anyone who would find it interesting to watch skin being shaved off their chest?'

'Me, for one,' Peggie observed, and grinned as Christopher stared at her in disbelief. 'It's probably got something to do with all the horror stories I liked to read when I was a kid. My heroes weren't Robin Hood, or William Tell, but Frankenstein and Darth Vader.'

'I told you the lady doctor was weird, didn't I?' Steven called out from his bed, and Christopher laughed and to Peggie's relief began to relax.

'You're using the power-driven dermatome to take Steven's grafts instead of the Humby?' Peggie observed with interest as Gareth selected it.

He nodded. 'It's more useful in this case. As all the grafts we'll be taking will be of the same thickness and width, the whole area should heal uniformly and I'll be able to come back to the donor site for more skin if I need to.'

'You make me sound like I'm some sort of take-away restaurant,' Christopher grumbled. 'And that thing you're going to use on me—it looks like something you'd make lasagne with.'

'It's not a bad comparison actually.' Gareth smiled. 'I can cut thin slices or thick just as a lasagne maker does. Sister Gilbert, did you remember to add—'

'1500 IU hyaluronidase to 100 ml of anaesthetic solution,' she and Peggie chorused together, and a deep tinge of colour appeared on Gareth's lean cheeks.

'It appears I'm getting predictable in my old age,' he said ruefully.

'Not predictable—just careful.' Sister Gilbert chuckled. 'If I was cutting grafts I'd want to add hyaluronidase to the anaesthetic too. It makes the grafts so much easier to cut.'

'Would you never advocate applying a local anaesthetic directly to the skin?' Peggie asked curiously as Gareth rubbed liquid paraffin onto Christopher's chest to enable the power-driven dermatome to operate more smoothly.

'It depends on the individual case,' he replied. 'EMLA— a mixture of lignocaine and prilocaine—is excellent be-

cause both agents are absorbed very slowly into the super-
ficial layers of the skin, with negligible absorption into the
blood stream, so you can anaesthetise a very large area.
The main problem is the anaesthesia might not extend to
the deeper part of the dermis so I wouldn't recommend
using it for anything other than thin or medium-thick grafts
and you must remember to wait at least an hour before you
start cutting.'

'Doesn't the colour of the skin gave you a good indication as to whether the anaesthetic has reached the parts
it should?' she commented.

'Usually, yes—' he nodded '—but it's not reliable
enough to take the risk. Now, Christopher, if you could just
lie back and relax for me...'

He was brilliant, Peggie thought as she watched Gareth
take graft after graft with apparent ease. His technique was
superb, his skill unquestionable. He might be a rat and a
louse when it came to personal relationships, but as a surgeon he was breathtaking.

'Told you skin grafts were nothing, didn't I?' Steven
shouted across when Gareth had carefully wrapped the last
of the grafts he'd taken in saline moistened gauze and Sister
Gilbert removed the screens round Christopher's bed.
'Now, if you want to know about a really difficult proce-
dure...'

'Children are amazingly resilient, aren't they?' Peggie
chuckled as she followed Gareth down the ward to the
sound of Steven's voice regaling Christopher with an in-
depth account of his operation. 'If I'd been through something as horrendous as Christopher or Steven, I'd just want
to pull the covers up over my head and hide.'

'It's easy to be resilient when they're cushioned in hospital from the outside world,' he murmured. 'It's later that
the emotional and psychological scars develop, and often...often those scars don't ever go away.'

He wasn't looking at her. He was lost in some private

world of his own, and she thought she'd never seen such pain and heartache in anybody's face before.

'Gareth, what it is—what's wrong?' she asked with concern.

He obviously didn't hear her and she put her hand on his arm only to see him suddenly blink and look round at her. 'I'm sorry, what did you just say?'

'Gareth—'

'The *very* man I'm looking for!' Frances Harper declared as she swung open the door of IC. 'And little Meggie, too— how *lovely*. Gary, you and I really *must* have a discussion about Christopher North's treatment.'

Now? Peggie thought, staring at the girl in disbelief. Gareth hadn't even applied Christopher's grafts yet so it was far too soon to be discussing the kind of exercises he might require to stop his skin tightening and restricting his movements.

It was obviously the best excuse Frances could come up with to spend some time in Gareth's company, and it was just as obvious that he desperately wanted rescuing.

A month ago she would have leapt to his aid without hesitation but now a malicious smile curved Peggie's lips.

'You have an hour free until your clinic this afternoon, don't you, Gary?' she said sweetly. 'So have fun, and I'll see you around, Fanny.'

And before either of them could reply she walked smartly out of IC and left him to Frances' mercy.

That would teach him to mess around with her, she thought as she headed for the canteen. She hoped Frances twisted his arm to go out with her and he had a really lousy time. Well, actually, no, if she was honest with herself, she didn't really want him dating the beautiful Ms Harper, but if Frances could perhaps make him squirm a lot as he tried to come up with some plausible excuses to get out of dating her she'd be delighted.

'Hey, Peggie, there's a seat free here at my table,' Jack

called the minute she went into the canteen. 'Come and join me.'

For a moment she hesitated, then nodded. OK, so Jack had behaved very badly over Sally but that was no reason for her to avoid him. They had to work together and despite everything she couldn't help liking him. He might be as much of a rat as Gareth when it came to personal relationships, but at least he was a very charming rat.

To her surprise, however, there wasn't much evidence of the anaesthetist's charm today. Jack talked about his work, about a particularly tricky Z-plasty operation Gareth had carried out, but all the time she felt he was ill at ease and uncomfortable.

'Jack, is something the matter?' she said eventually.

He bit his lip. 'I've got to talk to somebody, Peggie—if I don't, I'll go nuts.'

'You know you can talk to me,' she said encouragingly. 'I'm not a blabbermouth—I never have been.'

'I know,' he murmured. 'It's just…' A burst of laughter came from the doctors at the table behind them and he shook his head. 'Look, can we go somewhere quiet, private?'

'We could go to Marge's office,' she said with a slight frown. 'She'll be at lunch right now, but it isn't exactly the world's most comfortable place—'

'It'll do,' he said firmly, getting to his feet, his face pale but determined.

Curiouser and curiouser, she thought, as he led the way to the unit, but when they reached the receptionist's office and he began pacing the floor silently, clearly unsure of how to begin, she started to get really worried.

'Jack, are you in some kind of trouble?' she demanded eventually, unable to stand the suspense any longer.

He smiled a little crookedly. 'You could say that.'

'Look, if it's something to do with one of your many girlfriends I don't think I'm the best person in the world to talk to,' she murmured uncomfortably. 'Maybe you should talk to Tom—'

'There's no way I'm going to talk to Tom about this—no way!'

Her heart sank. 'Jack…Jack, have you got somebody pregnant?'

To her amazement a snort of bitter laughter came from him. 'That's the last thing I've done, believe me.'

'Then if it isn't girl trouble, what is it?' she said, bewildered.

'It is girl trouble, but not in the way you think,' he commented ruefully. 'Look, Peggie, a lot of what I say—in fact all of what I say about the girls in my life—it's…it's not true.'

'Pull the other one, Jack,' she protested. 'You've been out with practically every nurse who works at Lizzie's.'

He sat down opposite her with a deep sigh. 'Been out with—not gone to bed with.'

She gazed at him in surprise. 'But I thought…'

'So does everybody.' He laughed harshly. 'Jack Reid, the great Casanova, Jack Reid, every girl's dream guy. Jack Reid, the great wash-out.'

'But—'

'It's an act, Peggie. The talk, the chat, the flirting—it's all a big, phoney act. Why do you think I've dated so many women?'

Hot colour flooded into her cheeks. 'Because…well, because…I guess I thought you simply liked sex without commitment.'

'Peggie, I've never dated any woman more than four times in my life because after four dates most women are beginning to wonder why I haven't asked them to go to bed with me,' he declared.

'But—'

'Peggie…' He bit his lip and a deep tide of colour appeared on his cheeks. 'Peggie, the plain truth is I'm a twenty-eight-year-old virgin.'

'You're *what?*'

'For God's sake, keep your voice down,' he muttered, glancing nervously over his shoulder. 'Do you think I want everyone to know?'

'But why? I mean, it's none of my business why you...you haven't,' she added hurriedly, 'but—'

'Peggie, when I was young I had the worst case of facial acne you've ever seen. Boils, pimples—you name it, I had it. No girl at my school would have gone to the end of the road with me, far less out on a date.'

'But, Jack, you're a very handsome man now—'

'After years of dermabrasion maybe I am—' he sighed '—but inside I'm still the same old, gross Jack—the Jack girls used to laugh at and mock. Peggie, I've never made love to a woman because I'm terrified I might be rejected and laughed at like I was in the past.'

She stared at him silently, then cleared her throat.

'Jack, why are you telling me all this?' she asked softly, though in truth she felt she already knew the answer. 'Is it because you've met someone special? Jack, if it's Sally, tell her what you've just told me. She'll understand.'

'Tell her I'm a virgin?' He shook his head vehemently. 'Peggie, she'd laugh at me.'

'I don't think you understand women at all if you think she would laugh,' she said gently.

He shook his head again. 'There's no way I'm going to tell her—no way.'

'Then what are you going to do?' she protested. 'She thinks you've dumped her. If you don't talk to her, explain, you'll lose her. Jack, more problems and misunderstandings are caused by couples not talking than by anything else.'

'Maybe,' he said, 'but there has to be some other way I can deal with this other than telling her the truth. Look, I'm sorry, I shouldn't have burdened you with my problems,' he continued as she opened her mouth to argue with him. 'Especially as you've got problems of your own.'

She stiffened. 'Problems—I haven't got any problems.'

'Like you said—pull the other one,' he exclaimed.

'Jack, if I'm a bit down today it's only because it's my birthday, and I'm twenty-five, and still looking for Mr Right,' she replied lightly.

'Oh, come on, Peggie, you and I both know you've already found him,' he observed. 'So what's the problem?'

She wanted to deny it, to tell him he was wrong, but how could she when Jack had trusted her enough to tell her about himself? 'Jack…Jack, I think Gareth's married.'

His jaw dropped, then he started to laugh. 'Don't be ridiculous, Peggie. He can't possibly be married. If he was, you can bet your boots that hospital grapevine would not only know the day, the time, and even the register office he'd got married in, but also what colour her underwear was on the big day.'

'So how come a woman answered when I phoned his home last week?' she said unhappily.

'Because he's obviously got a cleaning lady, you idiot,' he declared.

'A cleaning lady who works until midnight, and who calls him darling?' She shook her head. 'I don't think so.'

'OK, so maybe he has a sister or some other female relative staying with him for a bit. Look, there's a simple way to find out. Ring up again, and if she answers, ask her.'

'I couldn't,' she gasped. 'If he found out it would look like I was chasing him.'

'Then why not just ask him straight out?'

'Because it would look as though I was interested,' she protested.

'But you are interested,' he exclaimed.

'Yes, but I don't want him to know that.'

He rolled his eyes heavenwards. 'You're right—I don't

understand women. Look, leave it to me, Peggie,' he continued as he got to his feet. 'I'll have a nose around and see what I can find out.'

'I'd be really grateful if you would,' she said as she accompanied him out of Marge's office, 'but—'

'I know, I know—' he nodded '—keep it under my hat. And thanks, Peggie.'

'I haven't done anything,' she declared.

'You listened, and you didn't laugh,' he said simply, and then suddenly, to her complete amazement, he pulled her into his arms.

'Jack—Jack, what the hell do you think you're doing?' she demanded, trying to extricate herself from his grasp.

'Stop struggling and play along with me,' he hissed into her ear.

'But—'

'Put your arms round my neck,' he muttered. 'Peggie, trust me—do as I say, and do it *now*.'

Totally bemused, she found herself doing exactly as he ordered, but after he'd kissed her soundly she gazed up at him in confusion.

'What was that all—?'

'Happy birthday, Peggie,' he said loudly, then quickly added under his breath, 'Don't move—stay right where you are—wait a minute, wait a minute—bingo!'

'OK, would you care to explain now what that little performance was all about?' she demanded when he released her.

His brown eyes danced. 'I was just giving God something to think about, that's all.'

She stared at him in total bewilderment then whirled round quickly in time to see Gareth's dark head disappearing down the corridor. 'Jack Reid, you are—'

'Brilliant—wonderful?' he suggested with a broad grin. 'Peggie, love, it won't do him one bit of harm to discover someone else finds you attractive.'

And as she began to laugh she rather thought it wouldn't.

She didn't feel much like laughing, however, by the time the last of her afternoon clinic had left at half-past six.

'I'm shattered.' She sighed as Angel placed the files of the patients she'd just seen in front of her. 'All I want to do is go home, have a hot shower, and go to bed, but I've still got all these damn files to collate.'

'Couldn't you leave them until tomorrow?' the staff nurse suggested.

Peggie shook her head. 'I'm in the operating theatre all morning, and I've another clinic in the afternoon. If I don't do them now I'll only have double to do tomorrow.'

'Well, I'm going home to put my feet up and if I'm really lucky maybe junior in here might stay still for five minutes,' Angel replied, rubbing her bump ruefully. 'Honestly, Peggie, if this baby doesn't become a footballer when he grows up, I'll eat my nurse's badge.'

Peggie laughed but as the staff nurse went out of the door she couldn't help sighing as she stared at the pile of files on her desk. Back home in Ireland she'd at least have had a huge birthday party to look forward to when she'd finished with this little lot, whereas now…

Now, all she had to look forward to was returning to an empty flat, to the leftover fish fingers from yesterday, and to whatever soap might be on TV.

'Stop feeling sorry for yourself, Peggie,' she muttered, picking up her pen. 'There are lots of people considerably worse off than you are, so just stop it.'

But by the time she had waded through the files her head was beginning to ache, her shoulders were screaming a protest, and she was feeling very sorry for herself indeed.

Wearily she pulled on her coat, switched off the light in her consulting room, and began walking down the corridor towards the elevators only to stop dead as a figure emerged from the shadows.

'Gareth, you almost gave me a heart attack!' she protested when she recognised him. 'I thought you'd gone home ages ago.'

'I was waiting for you.'

'Look, if it's about a patient—'

'It's not about a patient,' he interrupted. 'I was wondering if you'd like to come out with me tonight for dinner to celebrate your birthday?'

For a split second she was tempted—very tempted—until she remembered he probably hadn't realised it was her birthday until he'd heard Jack say it.

'Thanks for the offer,' she replied firmly, 'but all I really want to do is go home to bed.'

For an instant something flared in his eyes, then it was gone.

'Peggie, you can't not celebrate your birthday,' he exclaimed with a smile. 'They only come round once a year, remember.'

He was smiling that particular smile again. That smile that began at his lips and spread slowly into his eyes and she felt herself weakening.

He's probably intending to take you to Rosins again, a little voice whispered in her mind, and she stiffened.

She was not going to be influenced by that smile. OK, so her heart might have given that familiar little flip but she was not going to be influenced by that smile, or by those eyes, or by that damned aftershave of his.

'I'm sorry, but I really am tired, Gareth,' she declared, beginning to walk on. 'Perhaps some other time.'

Damn—why had she said that? She had never meant to say that, to give him the impression he could feel free to ask again.

'What about a drink, then?' he pressed. 'I know a very nice bar not very far from the hospital.'

Just like Rosins was not very far from the hospital, she thought as the elevator doors swung open and she stepped in. Not very far but just far enough away so he wouldn't meet anyone who might know him.

'I'd rather not, Gareth,' she replied. 'It's late.'

He glanced down at his watch. 'Half-past ten is late?'

'It's late, Gareth,' she repeated, pressing the button for the ground floor. 'Too late.'

And as the doors closed on him, a sad smile curved her lips as she caught sight of her reflection in the small mirror on the back wall of the elevator.

Her eyes looked huge and dark, her face pinched and white.

'Happy birthday, Peggie,' she murmured. 'Happy birthday.'

Chapter Eight

IT WAS hot in the city. It was quite unbearably hot in the hospital. Since the beginning of July they'd been sweltering under scorching temperatures and everyone at Lizzie's was feeling it.

Well, perhaps not quite everyone. Frances Harper wore crisp smart culottes and cool silk blouses and didn't look as though she knew the meaning of the word sweat.

'How the hell does she do it?' Sally exclaimed as the physiotherapist swung elegantly out of the unit after yet another lengthy discussion with Gareth about Christopher North's treatment. 'She hasn't a hair out of place, her mascara isn't even a little bit smudged, and the rest of us look like over-ripe tomatoes.'

'I know,' Peggie sighed, all too aware that her own hair was sticking to the back of her neck, her cheeks were quite unflatteringly flushed, and the blue cotton shirtwaister she was wearing was not only five years old but looked it.

'I just hope it gets a bit cooler by tonight or nobody's going to enjoy Angel's farewell party,' Sally declared. 'Did you remember to pick up her present—the vouchers for Belshey's Baby World?'

Peggie patted her handbag absently, her eyes following Gareth as he came out of his room and disappeared into Marge's office. 'I've got them here. Do you want them now?'

'Bring them with you tonight. You are still coming, aren't you?' Sally added with concern. 'You haven't changed your mind?'

'Of course I'm coming,' Peggie replied with as much enthusiasm as she could muster, and the staff nurse sighed.

'Look, I know you're still not happy about us holding the party at Rosins, but I thought it looked really nice when I dropped by last week, and let's face it—nobody else was prepared to give us a discount if we commandeered their whole restaurant.'

Privately Peggie didn't care if Rosins had been willing to give them the entire meal for nothing but she didn't say that.

'What did Gareth say when you told him we were holding the party at Rosins?' she said instead as she saw him coming out of the receptionist's office again.

'He seemed surprised—probably thought it might be a bit too pricey for us—but he didn't say anything.'

No, but I bet he gives Rosins a wide berth from now on, Peggie thought as he walked towards them.

'Ready for morning clinic, Peggie—Sally?' He smiled.

'I would be if you could get Admin to do something about the air-conditioning in here,' Sally replied. 'The heat's intolerable, Gareth.'

'I know,' he declared ruefully, 'but orthopaedics, IC, and the surgical and medical wards have a code one priority at the moment.'

'And what do we have—a code twenty-six?' Sally grumbled, but as Gareth walked away chuckling she muttered under her breath, 'It's all very well for him, Peggie. He's got his own electric fan. The rest of us have to make do with hanging around Marge's if we want a breath of air.'

He might well have his own fan but it certainly wasn't helping, Peggie thought as she stared after him. It was only half-past nine and yet already his shirt was sticking to his broad shoulders and muscular back.

Why the hell didn't he simply undo a few shirt buttons like everyone else instead of staying completely buttoned up? she wondered with irritation. She would quite happily have worn her theatre scrubs all day if she'd been allowed, and she had absolutely no sympathy for somebody who clearly thought he had an image to protect.

His image wasn't exactly uppermost in his mind when he took you home from Rosins that night, a little voice whispered at the back of her mind as she went into her consulting room. Any one of those nurses could quite easily have recognised him and it wouldn't have taken much imagination on their part to figure out what he was doing.

Oh, shut up, she told the annoying little voice. Just…just shut up. I refuse to think about him, or that night, ever again, OK?

So why haven't you told Jack to stop his Sherlock Holmes act? the annoying little voice asked. Why haven't you told him that it doesn't matter two hoots to you any more whether the mystery woman is Gareth's wife, or girl-friend, or just an extremely friendly housekeeper, because you're no longer interested?

Because the weak, wimpy part of me is still interested, she thought unhappily. The weak, wimpy part of me still cares a great deal.

'Then it's time you got a life, O'Neill,' she murmured as she put her handbag into her desk. 'It's time you stopped thinking about the man and accepted he's a louse.'

'Peggie?'

She whirled round, startled, and flushed.

How long had Gareth been standing there and, more to the point, could he have heard what she'd said?

'I did knock,' he said awkwardly as she stared at him in silence, 'but you clearly didn't hear me.'

'The heat must be affecting my ears as well as my brain,' she forced herself to say as lightly as she could. 'What can I do for you?'

For an instant she thought she saw something flare in his green eyes, then his expression became neutral, profes-sional.

'Tom is supposed to be helping me this afternoon with

the MacKenzie case—the little girl who was brought into A and E early this morning with a partially severed foot?'

'And there's a problem?' she queried.

He nodded. 'Some bigwig from the health board's on his way for an unscheduled visit and as I'd like him to see someone of seniority I wondered if you could assist me instead?'

She consulted her appointment book. 'What time's her operation?'

'Two o'clock.'

'It'll be tight,' she murmured. 'I've got mostly first-time consultations this morning, and they really can't be rushed. If I skip lunch—'

'Skip lunch?'

'I'll eat plenty tonight at Angel's party, believe me,' she said smoothly, seeing the frown in his eyes. 'Yes, I can assist you—no problem.'

He clearly wanted to say more but she didn't give him the opportunity. Deliberately she began sorting out the papers on her desk but when he walked slowly towards the door she could not help but shoot him a quick glance.

He looked tired. Tired, and drawn, and just a little bit sad.

Sympathy, O'Neill? her mind teased. I thought you weren't going to think about the man, and now you're worrying about him?

I am not, she retorted with as much conviction as she could, and heard the little voice at the back of her mind laugh mockingly.

'How are you getting to Angel's party tonight?' he asked suddenly. 'I could pick you up—'

'No need—I'm going with Sally,' she lied.

He fiddled with the door handle for a moment, then cleared his throat. 'I'll see you there, then.'

'I doubt it,' she declared, deliberately bright. 'With over

eighty people going I reckon most of us would be hard pressed to even find our own mothers.'

'Oh, I think I'd always manage to find you,' he said softly.

Her heart skipped a beat. There was warmth in his eyes—warmth, and a little sadness, and something else that made her pulses race. Stop it, Peggie, she told herself. Stop it. He's doing it again, playing games with you, and you're not going to play, remember?

Briskly she walked over to her filing cabinet and opened it with a bang. 'If there's nothing else, I really must get on, Gareth. My first patient's due in five minutes.'

Dimly she thought she heard him sigh but she didn't turn round. She just waited until she heard the door of her consulting room close then let out the breath she'd been unconsciously holding.

It'll get better with time, she reminded herself. Everything gets better with time.

Her morning sped by in a rush of consultations and it was almost a quarter to two by the time she'd finished seeing her last patient. So much for lunch. She had no time even for a cup of coffee and a biscuit.

'You're eating too much nowadays anyway, O'Neill,' she murmured, hurrying to the operating theatre and into one of the changing cubicles. 'And Gareth operates every day on an empty stomach.'

You're doing it again, she pointed out to herself as she stripped off her clothes and put on her theatre scrubs—thinking about him.

'Oh, go away and leave me in peace,' she exclaimed angrily.

'First sign of insanity, you know.' Jack grinned as she left the cubicle. 'Talking to yourself.'

'In that case I should have been certified years ago,' she replied. 'Has Fiona MacKenzie come up from IC?'

'She arrived fifteen minutes ago. We were just waiting for you before I put her under.' The anaesthetist glanced swiftly over his shoulder. 'Peggie, we need to talk. I've—'

'You made it,' Gareth exclaimed with clear relief, coming into the changing room. 'I was beginning to think your clinic must have seriously overrun. Jack, we're ready whenever you are.'

The anaesthetist hesitated, then nodded. 'Later, OK, Peggie?' he said in an undertone. 'We really do have to talk.'

Peggie's eyebrows rose as she followed him into the operating theatre but she didn't say anything. Hopefully all this secrecy meant Jack had finally decided he was going to tell Sally the truth about himself, but if he wanted advice on how to broach the subject she could only advise him to tell Sally exactly what he had told her.

With Fiona MacKenzie soon fast asleep, it didn't take Gareth long to align the operating microscope he was going to use to carry out the delicate task of sewing the little girl's foot back onto her leg.

'Fifteen years ago we couldn't even have attempted this,' he declared, noticing Peggie watching him. 'We could only have amputated but now we have a far better knowledge of the blood supply and—most importantly—the microsurgical tools for joining up very small blood vessels.'

'Don't you find it very disorientating—viewing the operation site through the binocular microscope instead of looking directly at it?' she asked. 'I know you can adjust the magnification and focus with the foot pedal, but you're still one step removed from the patient.'

'It's a bit like learning to ride a bicycle,' he observed. 'Once you've got the hang of the balance and co-ordination it's pretty plain sailing, really.'

A little voice told her that now was perhaps not the best time to tell him she'd never got the hang of learning to ride a bicycle.

'Instruments checked, Sally?' Gareth continued, turning to her.

'All present and correct, Gareth.'

'BP and heart-rate, Jack?'

'Couldn't be better. She's a very strong little girl.'

'OK, let's get to work,' he murmured.

He made it look so simple, Peggie thought as he began the delicate work of joining together the tiny severed nerves and equally small blood vessels in Fiona's leg and foot. As though doing something as intricate as this was commonplace instead of a miracle both of modern science and his own enormous skill.

One day, she vowed, she was going to be able to do operations like this. One day she was going to take a child who would have been disfigured for life and make her whole again.

It was a very weary team, however, which finally made their way into the changing room and shed their theatre scrubs, and Sally let out a groan as she looked at the time.

'It's half-past six already,' she exclaimed. 'The first guests are due to arrive at Rosins in a little over an hour, and I've still got a hundred and one things to do!'

'Can I help at all?' Peggie asked as Gareth left to hear how Tom had got on with the man from the health board.

'Would you?' Sally declared with relief. 'I haven't picked up Angel's flowers yet and—'

'Peggie, could I have a word?'

'Later, Jack, OK?' she replied as the anaesthetist joined them. 'Where did you order the flowers from, Sally?'

'Dunwoody downstairs. And if you could be an absolute angel—no pun intended,' the staff nurse continued, 'could you phone the restaurant for me and check that the band I booked is coming at nine o'clock and not ten?'

'Band?' Peggie gasped. 'Sally, there's never going to be enough room for eighty people to dance at Rosins.'

'Of course there will,' she replied airily. 'If they push the tables really far back—'

'What—out into the street?'

'Oh, ha ha, very funny. And when you phone the restaurant could you tell them we won't be needing a photographer after all— Sam Harrison says he'll do the honours.'

'Peggie, I really *do* want to talk to you,' Jack insisted.

'Not now,' she replied with irritation.

'But it's important—'

'And so is this,' she said firmly as she and Sally went out of the changing room, leaving the anaesthetist staring unhappily after them.

Rosins was crowded by the time Peggie arrived a little before eight and she had to admit that the manager had done a good job. Tables for six had been pushed as far back against the walls as was possible leaving an area in the middle of the restaurant for dancing, and there were flowers and banners everywhere proclaiming good wishes for Angel and her husband, Ian.

But as Peggie waved to David Chang and his wife, and mouthed a smiling hello to Daisy Swan and her boyfriend, her eyes weren't looking at the flowers or the banners but searching the crowd for the sight of one particular man.

Once—oh, it seemed so long ago now—she'd been amazed to find herself thinking Gareth was an attractive man, but now, when she caught sight of him dressed in a plain blue shirt and casual black trousers, the only thing that amazed her was why it wasn't obvious to everyone that he was quite the best-looking man in the room.

Frances Harper clearly agreed with her. Frances who was hanging possessively onto his arm and whose interpretation of the instruction 'Dress casual' appeared to be a stunning cream lace dress which showed off her slender figure to perfection.

Peggie sighed as she gazed down at her own plain red

cotton dress with its button-through, puffed-sleeved bodice
and wide skirt. She wished she could have bought something new for tonight. She wished even more that there was
a shop which sold dresses which instantly made you look
like a size twelve, or even a fourteen.

'I thought you were never coming!' Sally gasped as she
pushed her way through the throng, looking very pretty in
a camisole pink top and short blue skirt. 'Did you remember the flowers?'

'They're outside in the hall. I thought they'd stand less
chance of wilting if I left them there,' Peggie replied.

'Smart thinking.' Sally nodded. 'Your table's over there,'
she continued, pointing to the far end of the room. 'I put
you with Sam Harrison and his wife, and Lucas and
Claudia. I...I hope that's OK?' she added a little uncertainly.

'Fine,' Peggie declared, dredging up a smile.

And it was fine, she told herself. The last person she
wanted to sit next to all night was Gareth Davies. Of course
it was.

The meal was excellent, the company at her table
couldn't be faulted, and by eleven o'clock Peggie could
have boasted she'd danced with almost every head of department in Lizzie's. Every one, that was, except for the
head of Plastic Surgery.

Considering you can't even stand next to the man in the
operating theatre without your heart going crazy, it's probably just as well, she told herself. And yet she could not
help sighing as Claudia and Lucas danced by, just back
from their honeymoon, and so obviously very much in love.

'Peggie, can I talk to you *now*?' Jack declared, appearing
without warning at her table with the look of a man determined not to be fobbed off.

'Of course you can.' She smiled absently, tapping her
foot to the beat of the music.

'Peggie, it's Gareth. I've found out something about Gareth.'

Her foot stilled. The anaesthetist's face looked pale in the restaurant's dimmed lighting—pale and unhappy—and her heart faltered.

'I'm not going to like it, am I?' she murmured.

He shook his head and she suddenly noticed that Gareth was weaving his way through the crowded dance floor towards her. Within seconds he would be at her table. Within seconds he was probably going to ask her to dance.

'Jack, can't it wait?' she said quickly.

'I don't think it can,' he replied, seeing the direction of her gaze.

'But—'

'Please, Peggie,' he said softly.

She didn't want to hear what he had to say. She wanted this one dance with Gareth, and yet as Jack tugged gently at her arm she got to her feet and followed him out into the quiet of the restaurant corridor.

'I…I think I can guess what you're going to say,' she said when Jack stood silently for a moment, clearly uncertain on how to begin. 'He's married with three children, isn't he?'

The anaesthetist sighed. 'I'm afraid it's worse than that, Peggie.'

'How much worse can a wife and three children be?' she exclaimed.

A dull flush of colour appeared on Jack's cheeks. 'Peggie, I think…I'm sorry, but I think he's gay.'

She stared at him, open-mouthed for a moment, then a peal of laughter broke from her. 'That's the most ludicrous thing I've ever heard. Gareth can't—'

'Peggie, I've been snooping around like I promised,' he interrupted, 'and last weekend I saw him coming out of his flat with a woman.'

'Then he's married like I said,' she protested.

Jack shook his head. 'I couldn't see her face—she was all muffled up—but I could tell by the way she walked that she wasn't a young woman so I asked around in the local shops. He lives with his mother, Peggie.'

'So he lives with his mother,' she retorted. 'That doesn't mean he's gay.'

'Peggie, he's thirty-six years old, he's never dated one single woman in the three years he's been at Lizzie's, and he lives with his mother. Doesn't that tell you something?'

'But—'

'If you need any further proof look at Frances Harper,' he continued. 'The woman drools all over him every time they meet and yet he's always knocked her back. Now, whatever else you might say about Frances she's one stunning-looking girl, and you're not telling me Gareth isn't bright enough to get her into bed with him without finding himself walking down the aisle afterwards. If he's not gay, what's his problem?'

It made sense, she thought, staring at him with dismay. The one time Gareth had kissed her he had backed off, not her. He'd said it was because he felt relationships between colleagues didn't work, but maybe the real truth was he simply preferred men.

'Peggie—oh, Peggie, love, don't!' Jack said with concern as she started to laugh.

'Why not?' she demanded, knowing that if she didn't laugh she was undoubtedly going to cry. 'It's so funny, don't you see? So very, very funny.'

He grabbed her by the shoulders and gave her a little shake. 'Peggie, if you don't stop this right now, I swear I'll slap you!'

'I wouldn't advise it,' an icy voice exclaimed from the end of the corridor. 'Not unless you're planning on having some extensive plastic surgery of your own!'

Gareth was walking towards them, his face grim, and

Jack coloured uncomfortably. 'It's not how it looks, boss. Peggie…Peggie's a little upset, that's all.'

'I can see that,' he said tightly. 'What I want to know is why?'

'It's nothing—really, it's nothing,' she insisted, wiping the tears of laughter from her eyes quickly.

'You crying is nothing?' he demanded.

She opened her mouth to tell him that she hadn't been crying only to bite back the words. How could she say she hadn't been crying but laughing at the irony of having fallen in love with a man who was gay? Somehow she didn't think he would find it funny, and judging by his taut expression and clenched fists, if she didn't do something fast Jack was going to be in big trouble.

'I'd like to talk to Gareth on my own, if you don't mind, Jack,' she said swiftly.

'But, Peggie—'

'Please,' she begged, and after a moment's hesitation the anaesthetist sighed and shook his head.

'OK, but if you need me, you know where I am,' he murmured, making for the restaurant door.

'And if I discover you're the cause of Peggie's tears, Jack,' Gareth said grimly, 'I'll know where to find you too!'

Peggie swallowed hard as the restaurant door swung shut and Gareth stared down at her clearly waiting for an explanation. What was it she had told Jack? That more problems and misunderstandings were caused by people not talking than by anything else? Well, now it was time to take a leaf out of her own book.

'Gareth…' She paused and swallowed again. 'Gareth, why didn't you tell me the truth when you said you and I could never get involved?'

His black eyebrows snapped down. 'Is that why you were crying?'

She flushed slightly. 'Jack…he's just told me about you.

About why you don't date. About…about your circum-
stances.'

'How the hell did he find out?' he demanded.

So it was true, she thought miserably. She'd hoped he
would deny it, tell her what Jack had said was ridiculous—
ludicrous—but he hadn't.

'Does it matter how he found out?' she murmured.
'Look, I might come from a quiet rural area, but things like
this…situations like this…it's not unheard of.'

'Situations?' he echoed with a slight frown. 'I wouldn't
exactly call my life a situation.'

The colour on her cheeks deepened. She was making an
unholy mess of this, she knew she was.

'Gareth—'

'Sorry to interrupt you both,' Sally exclaimed as she clattered into the corridor, 'but it's time for you to make
Angel's presentation, Gareth.'

He went with clear reluctance and Peggie didn't follow
him. She had no desire now to celebrate anything. After
Jack's revelation all she wanted was to go home.

But the minute the taxi dropped her off at her flat she
wished she was back at the party. At the party laughter and
music could have shut out the thoughts that kept crowding
into her mind, in her quiet flat there were no diversions to
distract her.

How could she have been so stupid, so naive? she wondered as she curled up in a seat and hugged her knees. Sally
had told her once that she believed Gareth would have been
happier if he could have staffed his entire department with
men. How could she not have realised why?

No one else has realised, she reminded herself when she
heard the sound of someone knocking insistently on her
door. Nobody else suspects, she told herself as she wearily
went to answer it, but when she opened the door and saw
Gareth standing there her professional instincts immediately clicked into place.

'Is my pager not working—my phone?' she exclaimed, reaching for her bag. 'Give me a second to put on my shoes and I'll be—'

'Relax, Peggie,' he interrupted. 'I'm not here because there's an emergency at the hospital.'

'Then…?'

'You can't tell me you know why I don't date, call my life ''a situation'', and then disappear into the night without another word.'

She flushed. 'Gareth—'

'Are you going to invite me in, or are we going to have this conversation on your doorstep?'

'I'm sorry—please, please come in,' she said, stepping back quickly. 'Sit down, make yourself comfortable.'

His eyes swept round the bedsitting-cum living room taking in the clothes strewn on the bed, the underwear draped over the backs of the only two chairs, and the books and papers scattered on the floor.

'Did you have any particular area in mind?' he asked wryly.

She coloured even more.

'I'm sorry, my flat doesn't usually look this bad,' she declared, hurriedly sweeping up the underwear and clothes, and shoving them haphazardly into her wardrobe. 'But I've been on emergency stand-by three nights in a row, and—'

'Peggie, I'm not a member of the neatness squad sent round by the board to assess you,' he said gently.

She bit her lip. He must think she was an idiot—she was certainly behaving like one—but he was the last person in the world she'd expected to see.

'Would you like a coffee, a cup of tea?' she asked in desperation.

He grimaced. 'In this heat?'

'What about a glass of wine, then?' she offered, diving under the bed and emerging rather breathlessly with a bottle.

'That's your fridge?' he said, eyeing the bed and the bottle uncertainly.

'We don't have fridges of our own. Each floor has a shared kitchen, and the wine was a present for my birthday from my Uncle Sean and I meant to put it in the fridge—' She stopped abruptly. 'Look, if you'd rather not bother—'

'I'm sure it will taste wonderful,' he lied.

Hurriedly she dived under the bed again, resurfaced with two pottery mugs, and splashed a liberal amount of wine into them.

'I'm sorry about the mug,' she murmured uncomfortably as she handed him one. 'I've always meant to buy some glasses—'

'Will you stop apologising, and just relax?' he insisted.

She wished she could. She wished she'd never left the party. And she wished with all her heart that she were a million miles away from here.

'You weren't lying when you said you had a copy of my book,' he observed, putting down his mug after only one sip and picking up the well-thumbed copy of *The Fundamental Principles of Plastic Surgery* at his feet.

'Why in the world would I lie?' she asked in confusion.

'Why, indeed?' He nodded. 'So perhaps now you'll tell me what you meant by saying that situations like mine aren't unheard of in rural Ireland?'

She put down her mug, wondering if the wine in it really did taste as awful as she thought it did, and pulled herself together. She was going to be adult about this if it killed her.

'What I said—I phrased it very badly. What I meant to say was that I understand now—because…because of the genes you were born with—why friendship is all you can ever offer me.'

'The genes I was born with?' he echoed, clear confusion appearing on his face.

'It's nothing to be ashamed of,' she continued doggedly.

'Good grief, I doubt if anyone would even raise an eyebrow nowadays if you told them.'

'Raise an eyebrow?' he repeated.

'Absolutely.' She nodded vigorously. 'In fact…in fact, coming out is becoming really fashionable now.'

'Coming out?' he said faintly.

'Politicians are doing it all the time, and pop stars—'

'My God, you think I'm *gay!*'

'Gareth—'

'You honestly believe after the way I kissed you, after we almost— What the hell makes you think I'm gay?' he exclaimed, not knowing whether he wanted to laugh or throttle her.

'I knew—I thought—you liked me,' she said, crimsoning deeply, 'but every time we got close you seemed to back away. It's common knowledge at Lizzie's that you've never been married, you don't go out on dates, and when Jack told me you lived with your mother—'

'You put two and two together and came up with twenty-five.' He groaned. 'I'm surprised you stopped at deciding I was gay. Why not make me bisexual, or transsexual, or a transvestite who likes dressing up in women's clothes?'

'You don't, do you?' she faltered. 'Not that it's any of my business if you do,' she continued hurriedly as he got to his feet, his face furious. 'I mean lots of people probably do the same—well, maybe not lots—'

'God give me strength!' he roared. 'It's a wonder the staff at Lizzie's ever get round to treating any patients, the amount of time they spend speculating on people's private lives! Just because I've never married and don't date doesn't automatically make me gay, and I do *not* live with my mother. My mother lives with me and has done since my father died three years ago because…well, because she can't cope on her own.'

She gazed at him uncertainly. 'Are you…are you saying you're not gay?'

For an answer he pulled her to her feet and his lips came down on hers with a kiss that took her breath away.

She'd thought she'd felt the full force of his passion that night in his car but this—this was something else. His mouth was fierce, demanding, bruising her lips and throat, and though she wanted him—her thundering heart told her that—she didn't want him like this. She didn't want him to make love to her in anger, to prove a point.

'Gareth…please…' she gasped, struggling protestingly against the iron band of his arms, and to her surprise he released her immediately.

'I'm sorry—so sorry,' he muttered, his breathing ragged, his voice thick and husky. 'I won't…not like that…not like that.'

She thought he was leaving and put out a hand to stop him, but he wasn't leaving. Instead he cupped her face between fingers that shook and forced her to look up at him.

'Peggie, I'm not gay. God help me, but there have been times when I've wished I'd been born a eunuch, but I am definitely not gay.'

His voice sounded choked, and she could see the pulse-beat hammering in his throat.

'Gareth—'

'I want you, Peggie O'Neill. I want you so much it's tearing me apart.'

She could see the desire in his eyes, feel it in the trembling fingers that cupped her face, and she smiled a little tremulously.

'And I want you, Gareth Davies,' she whispered, and this time when his lips came down on hers they were the lips of her dreams—gentle, coaxing, teasing.

He didn't hold her, he didn't even attempt to touch her at all, and it was her hands which eventually slid up his broad back to twine themselves around his neck, her body that moved closer to his, moulding herself to his taut, muscular frame.

He groaned and deepened the kiss, easing her lips apart, delving deep into her mouth so that she convulsed against him.

'Hold me, Gareth...please...please, hold me,' she begged into his neck, and only then did he wrap his arms around her, only then did he lift her to him so that she knew that when he'd said he wanted her it had been no lie.

Very soon mere kisses were not enough. Very soon her dress had been discarded along with her bra and pants, but when she stood naked before him he swallowed convulsively.

'God, but you are so beautiful, Peggie,' he said hoarsely.

'I'm not,' she faltered, overwhelmingly embarrassed by his intense scrutiny. 'I'm too short, too fat, too...too...'

'Self-critical,' he said with a strange, almost self-mocking smile as he switched off the light.

'Gareth, where are you?' she protested, taking a blind step forward and almost falling over a chair. 'Let me at least put on the bedside—'

Her protest was swallowed up by his lips. Lips that now were no longer gentle but hungry, and hands that stroked and caressed and tantalised so that when he laid her on the bed her one desire was for him never to stop kissing and touching her.

Feverishly she plucked at his shirt, at the waistband of his trousers, wanting to feel his body, to touch him too, but he captured her hands in his and pulled them up over her head, imprisoning her.

She moaned as he took first one taut nipple into his mouth and then the other and suckled them gently, but when his lips slid down to taste the already damp curls between her legs she writhed beneath him, her body begging for release.

He moved away from her briefly and desperately she called out his name, heedless of who might hear her, only to gasp and wince when he suddenly slid into her. She heard his own sharp intake of breath and for one frustrating moment she thought he was actually going to stop, and then he imprisoned her hands again and began to move within her, slowly at first then faster, until she forgot all about the pain, forgot about everything, and her hips rose up to meet him.

Tentatively at first and then with more confidence she began to follow his rhythm, her body echoing his every thrust, until deep within her a feeling began to grow, a sensation that spiralled and spiralled until she convulsed and cried out again but this time in ecstasy.

He reached his own climax seconds later but as she drifted into sleep, still wrapped in his arms, she could not help but wonder why, at the moment of his greatest pleasure, he should lay his head on her breast and murmur her name over and over again as though he had lost something and not gained it.

Chapter Nine

IT WAS the sound of Brian Wilson's cheerful whistling as he headed off for his early morning shift in Ophthalmics that awoke Peggie with a start. For a second she couldn't quite recall where she was and then a wide smile curved her lips as she saw her clothes scattered on the floor and remembered how they'd got there.

Carefully she eased herself round, wincing slightly at the unaccustomed tenderness between her legs, but Gareth wasn't lying beside her. He was sitting on a chair, his eyes closed, and she smiled again. His clothes weren't scattered all around the floor. He had wanted her so very badly last night that he hadn't even taken the time to fully undress, but this morning....

She glanced at her bedside clock. They had an hour yet before they had to leave for work. An hour during which she fully intended to see for herself whether his chest really was as broad as it had felt beneath her fingers a few hours ago.

Carefully she raised herself up onto her pillow but he must have heard her slight movement because his eyes suddenly snapped open.

'Not fair, Mr Modesty,' she murmured, smiling shyly across at him. 'You've seen my figure, warts and all, but I—'

'Why didn't you tell me you were a virgin?'

She blinked. Of all the things she'd expected him to say after last night, this certainly wasn't one of them.

'Does it matter?' she said in confusion.

'Of course it bloody well matters,' he exclaimed, his face

taut, his eyes furious. 'A woman of your age shouldn't still be a virgin!'

Hot colour crept over her cheeks and she pulled her duvet protectively around her. 'You make it sound like I was suffering from some awful incurable disease,' she protested. 'Well, I'm not a virgin any more, so you should be happy now.'

'Happy?' He spat out the word, then swore under his breath. 'Peggie, don't you see that it makes everything so much harder—so much more complicated?'

She gazed at him in confusion. 'What does it make harder? Gareth…Gareth, are you trying to tell me you're married?'

'Of course I'm not married!' he retorted.

'Then you're not making any sense,' she exclaimed. 'What's so terrible about us making love? Are you saying it would have been all right if I'd been experienced—if I hadn't been a virgin?'

'Yes—no!' He got to his feet jerkily and raked his hands through his black hair. 'Oh, God, this is such a mess—such a bloody awful mess. You should have *told* me, Peggie!'

'What was I supposed to do?' she demanded. 'Go about with a sign over my head saying "Caution—My name's Peggie O'Neill—and I'm a virgin"! If I'd known you were going to make such a big deal about it I'd have asked one of the window cleaners or the janitors to make love to me first!'

He bit his lip. 'You don't understand. Your first time shouldn't have been with me. It should have been with someone with whom you could have had a future.'

Was he saying they didn't have a future? Did he mean that even after making love to her nothing had changed?

'Gareth—'

'You've got this afternoon off, haven't you?' he interrupted.

'You know I have—you make up the rosters. I've a clinic

this morning, and then I'm helping you with Liam Docherty's op at one o'clock—'

'I'll pick you up at three. There's something you have to know. Something I should have told you a long time ago.'

'Gareth, you're still not making any sense,' she said in confusion, reaching for her dressing gown. 'Can't you just tell me now?'

He shook his head. 'This afternoon. You'll know everything this afternoon.'

'Where are you going?' she exclaimed as he suddenly walked to the door.

'Home to shower and change.'

'But, Gareth—'

He didn't even turn round. He just slammed out and as she heard the sound of his footsteps growing fainter and fainter in the corridor outside she hugged her arms tightly across her chest. Last night should have been the most wonderful night of her life, and it had been until now. It had been until Gareth had opened his deep green eyes and looked at her and she'd seen an expression of absolute horror in them.

'Fiona's doing fine—absolutely fine,' Sam Harrison declared reassuringly, understanding plain in his face as Peggie gazed at him uncertainly. 'It's far too early yet to say if we'll have any problems with rejection, but, like we say in the trade, at the moment she's comfortable.'

Peggie sighed with relief. She'd started thinking about Fiona MacKenzie the minute she'd left her flat, and as soon as she'd started thinking she'd known there was no way she was going to be able to get through her shift until she'd found out if the girl was all right.

'I see Steven and Christopher are still as chatty as ever,' she observed, gesturing to the two boys who were deep in a heated discussion about the relative merits of various football teams.

Sam groaned as he accompanied her to the door. 'I'll be delighted when the pair of them can be transferred down to Surgical so I can get a bit of peace and quiet.'

She laughed but as she turned to go the consultant quickly caught hold of her arm.

'Not so fast, Dr O'Neill,' he declared, his eyes sparkling. 'You're not going anywhere until you tell me what was going on between you and Gareth last night.'

'Going on?' she repeated, deliberately casual, though she could feel a warm blush of colour creeping across her cheeks. 'Nothing was going on, Sam.'

'So how come he spent half an hour asking everyone at the party where you'd gone then went off with a face like thunder never to return?' He shook his head. 'You'll have to come up with something better than that, Peggie.'

'Much as it grieves me to disappoint you, Sam,' she said with a calmness she was very far from feeling, 'we simply had a minor disagreement about our operating schedule this morning.'

'Your operating schedule?' he repeated.

'You know what Gareth's like—never stops thinking about work even at a party,' she replied, quite happily perjuring her soul and reinforcing Gareth's reputation as a kill-joy at one stroke. 'But it's all sorted out now.'

The consultant looked seriously disappointed, then rallied. 'What about Sally and Jack, then? When you left the party they were getting very friendly. Are they back together again, or what?'

'Your guess is as good as mine,' she said lightly, then shook her head. 'No—I take that back. Your guess would undoubtedly be considerably more colourful if not as accurate as mine. And now I really must go, Sam,' she continued as he opened his mouth, clearly itching to delve deeper. 'I've got a clinic and I don't want to be late.'

'You know something, Peggie O'Neill,' he called after her. 'You're about as much use as a train timetable when it comes to interesting information.'

'And you are nothing but an old gossip, Sam Harrison,' she called back, 'and if you're looking for juicy titbits of information I'm afraid you'll need to find another source.'

She could still hear his laughter as she went up the stairs but she didn't feel remotely like laughing.

If it was true that Jack and Sally were getting on well together again, then that was very good news, but the last thing she wanted was the rumour factory turning its attention to her and Gareth. To have any chance of a future together—and judging by Gareth's words this morning it was an almost non-existent chance—rumour and speculation were the last thing they needed.

But, as Peggie very quickly discovered, the rumour factory had already been busily at work.

'Hey, Peggie, you and Gareth must really have had a humdinger of a row at the party last night,' Marge protested the minute she saw her. 'Do you know what he told me when I said Mrs Drew wanted him to interview some candidates for Angel's job this afternoon?'

'No, but I'm sure you're going to tell me,' Peggie said dryly.

'He said it was his afternoon off and he wasn't going to spend it hanging around the hospital interviewing bloody nurses. And bloody's his word, not mine.'

'Marge, it's surely not beyond the realms of possibility that he actually has made some personal plans for this afternoon?' Peggie exclaimed.

'Personal plans—Gareth? The man doesn't have a personal life. He eats, sleeps, and breathes work. Look, this row you had—'

'Sorry, Marge, but I have to go,' Peggie interrupted quickly, seeing Sally coming down the corridor to join her for the start of her morning clinic, but any relief she might have felt at the staff nurse's appearance was destined to be short-lived.

The minute she and Sally were alone the girl took her hand comfortingly in hers.

'Peggie, Jack told me all about Gareth last night and I'm so very sorry.'

'Sorry about what?' Peggie said, momentarily thrown.

'About him being gay, of course.'

Peggie didn't know whether to laugh or cry and opted for the former. 'Sally, Gareth isn't gay.'

The staff nurse sighed. 'Peggie, denial's not good. I know you want it to be otherwise but avoiding the issue, running away from it—'

'Sally, I don't care what Jack told you, Gareth isn't gay,' Peggie protested, wishing the anaesthetist were here in person so she could stick pins in him—lots of large ones—for telling the staff nurse anything. 'Last night—'

'Was deeply upsetting for you—I know that,' the staff nurse finished for her, 'but putting your head in the sand—'

'Oh, I'm sorry, I thought you were alone, Peggie,' Gareth apologised as he swung into her room.

Chance would be a fine thing, she thought grimly. Right now she felt like one of the victims of the Spanish Inquisition awaiting the arrival of yet another torturer.

'Is it important, Gareth?' she asked wearily. 'Because if it's not…'

He stared at her uncertainly for a moment, then shook his head. 'It'll keep.'

'You know, I never would have guessed,' Sally said wonderingly, the minute he had gone. 'I mean, I know he doesn't date or anything, but he looks every inch the macho man—'

'Enough!' Peggie roared, driven beyond endurance. 'Sally, Gareth is *not* gay. Nor is he bisexual, transsexual, or a transvestite,' she continued as the girl opened her mouth, clearly intending to argue. 'And I'll tell you something else,' she continued, her brown eyes grim. 'If I hear one word—even the merest whisper—around the hospital about Gareth's sexuality I'm going to know exactly who to come to—aren't I?'

The staff nurse gulped. 'I won't say a word, I promise.'

'And Jack better not either,' Peggie continued, opening her appointment book with a snap, 'because if he does you can tell him from me that I'll make him wish he'd never been born!'

'You were so right, Dr O'Neill,' Mrs Turner beamed, relief and pleasure equally mixed on her plump face. 'Even I can see the difference in Kate's face now. The port-wine stain's scarcely visible at all.'

'I told you I felt sure it was only a question of time, didn't I?' Peggie smiled.

'I know you did but, you see, part of me wouldn't allow myself to believe it in case it didn't happen,' Mrs Turner confessed. 'I didn't want to face the disappointment.'

Peggie nodded understandingly as she gently turned Kate's face into the light to examine her cheek.

The haemangioma was looking good. It was looking very good indeed. The endothelial cells of the vessels which had caused the little girl's port-wine stain were definitely atrophying and, with luck, one more treatment should be enough to eradicate it completely.

'OK, Kate, could you—?'

'Put on the goggles and keep as still for you as I can while you shine the torch in my cheek,' the girl intoned and Peggie laughed.

'You're getting quite an expert at this, aren't you?' she said, slipping the goggles carefully over the child's head.

'I want to be a doctor like you when I grow up,' Kate replied. 'A doctor who can give people new faces and make them happy.'

'Then I wish you every success, sweetheart.' Peggie

smiled as she put on her own goggles. 'It's not an easy road, by any means. You'll have to study really hard, and face lots of set-backs, but if you make it I can tell you it's the best job in the world.'

And it was, Peggie thought as her morning sped by in a whirl of referrals and assessments. Despite all her current problems she wouldn't have swopped her profession for anything.

'Last patient coming up, Peggie,' Sally announced at half-past twelve. 'Billy Oswald for you to check on the results of his otoplasty op.'

It only needed one look at Mr and Mrs Oswald's smiling faces to tell Peggie that the operation had been a complete success.

'We can't thank you enough, Doctor,' Mrs Oswald declared as her husband nodded his agreement. 'I know some people would see it as vanity—that Billy should just have accepted what the good Lord gave him—but having his ears pinned back—it's made such a difference to his life, hasn't it, Billy?'

The little boy smiled shyly up at Peggie. 'I brought you a present, Doctor. A picture I drew of me before the operation, and a picture of me after it.'

She gazed down at the drawings he was holding out to her and tears pricked at the backs of her eyes. One picture was of a little boy standing alone, his ears huge caricatures, while the other showed the same little boy surrounded by lots of friends, his ears no more than tiny shells on either side of his head.

'It's lovely,' she murmured. 'I'll treasure it always, thank you.'

And she would, she knew as Billy and his parents left. Having your ears pinned back wasn't perhaps the most radical or difficult of operations, but for one little boy it had made the world seem a brighter and less unhappy place, and for that alone it had been worthwhile.

'Ready for Liam Docherty's op?' Gareth asked as she left her consulting room.

'As I'll ever be,' she replied.

'Peggie—'

'Did I see Wendy Arnold—the girl who had part of her ear bitten off—in the waiting room earlier?' she interrupted quickly, not wishing to argue with him again as to whether Liam should be having his operation at all.

He nodded. 'She came in for a check-up.'

'How's she doing?' she asked, following him out of the unit and up the stairs towards the operating theatre.

'There's some slight scarring behind her ear where I swung the skin-cartilage sandwich over and re-attached it, but once I've applied a small skin graft it should be virtually identical to her other ear.'

'You must be pleased,' she observed.

'It's always very satisfying when you try something different and it works.' He paused and glanced down at her. 'And talking about doing something different, you haven't forgotten about this afternoon, have you?'

'Of course I haven't,' she replied. 'I just wish you'd stop all this cloak and dagger stuff and tell me now.'

'Later, OK, Peggie,' he murmured as they passed Sam Harrison on the stairs and the consultant stopped to stare speculatively after them. 'I'll tell you later.'

There was no point in pressing him. She knew it was useless and with a sigh she followed him into the changing room, only to stop dead on the threshold when she saw Jack waiting for them.

Quickly she glanced across at Gareth. He hadn't seen the anaesthetist since last night. What would he say to him? Would he lambast Jack for telling her he was gay, or pretend she hadn't told him?

To her dismay an unholy gleam appeared for a second in Gareth's eyes, then he walked quickly across to the anaesthetist.

'Everything ready for the operation, Jack?' he asked.

'Absolutely—no problems at all, Gareth,' he replied, shooting Peggie a questioning glance, but she couldn't help him. She had no idea what was going through Gareth's mind.

'Good—good.' Gareth beamed, and then completely without warning he suddenly placed an arm around Jack's shoulders and gave him a hug. 'I know I can always rely on my very favourite anaesthetist.'

'Yes—well—that's nice to hear,' Jack exclaimed in strangled tones, wriggling free from Gareth's grasp, his cheeks considerably flushed. 'Now, if you'll excuse me…'

He all but ran from the changing room and the minute the door slammed behind him Peggie let out a peal of laughter. 'Oh, Gareth, you shouldn't have done that—you really shouldn't!'

'I know.' He chuckled.

'You're not going to let him go around thinking you're gay, are you?' she protested. 'What if he tells somebody?'

'He won't, and I'll tell him the truth in a couple of days.'

'You promise?' she insisted.

He nodded. 'I promise, but, believe me, I'm going to make him very, very nervous for the next few days.'

She laughed again. 'Gareth, about this afternoon…'

All amusement disappeared from his face in an instant. 'Peggie, I wish things were different. I truly wish we could have a future together, but all the wishing in the world can't make it so.'

She took a step towards him but he put up his hands defensively and backed away.

'No, Peggie,' he murmured hoarsely. 'This afternoon… This afternoon you'll see why it can never be.'

He would never make her believe that, she thought as he disappeared into one of the changing cubicles. There was nothing he could say that would be so awful that it would make her stop loving him. She loved him now, and she knew she always would.

Liam Docherty's parents had agreed that it would be less stressful for their son if his Down's syndrome appearance could be altered in stages rather than by subjecting him to the ordeal of what would otherwise have been at least a four hour operation. But to correct the slant in his eyes, pin back his ears, and make his nose less flat by reshaping the bone and cartilage took time—a lot of time.

'OK, if you'd suture under Liam's eyes for me, Peggie, I think we've finally got a wrap,' Gareth said when he eventually wearily straightened up from the operating table.

Quickly she took his place, surreptitiously rotating her own shoulders to try to ease the stiffness between them, but as she began suturing the cuts under the little boy's eyes Kate Turner's words suddenly came back into her mind.

'I want to be a doctor…who can give people new faces and make them happy,' she'd said.

Wasn't that exactly what Liam Docherty's parents wanted for their son?

If she'd been in Gareth's position, Liam's operation would never have taken place. But did she have the right to withhold her surgical skills and thereby subject a little boy to a lifetime of taunts and assumptions by others based purely on his appearance? She might have the dubious pleasure of occupying the high moral ground on the issue, but wasn't Gareth's position the more realistic?

It was almost a quarter to three before Liam was finally wheeled into Recovery and as Peggie came out of her changing cubicle Gareth glanced ruefully up at the clock.

'I'm afraid we're going to have to leave straight from the hospital.'

'Leave?' she repeated in confusion. 'Gareth, when you said you were going to explain everything you didn't mention anything about having to go somewhere to do it.'

'I don't think my mother would be willing to come to the hospital—'

'Your mother—you're taking me to meet your mother?' she gasped, gazing down in dismay at her badly creased green cotton shirtwaister. 'Gareth, I can't go like this. Give me a quarter of an hour to go home and change—'

'We haven't got time. My mother always visits a friend on Friday afternoons and if we don't hurry, we'll miss her.'

'But—'

He wasn't even listening to her. He was already at the door and she followed him belligerently. Why couldn't he have told her this morning that he was taking her to meet his mother? She could easily have brought a change of clothes into the hospital with her, but now, instead of hopefully impressing the mother of the man she loved, she would arrive looking a crumpled wreck.

And not just a crumpled wreck but completely lost, she thought, when Gareth turned his car east and kept on driving.

'You thought I lived in one of those smart executive flats near Regent's Park or maybe in one of those large houses in Kensington, didn't you?' He smiled across at her, clearly sensing her bewilderment.

'Well, yes,' she admitted. 'So where do you live?'

'Out past Battersea.'

'Battersea?' she echoed faintly.

He glanced across at her with some amusement. 'Peggie, my parents owned a few acres of the worst agricultural land in Wales. I went to med school on a scholarship, lived on beans and sausages most terms, and was the butt of every joke because of my second-hand clothes. Believe me, Battersea is more my kind of area than Kensington or Regent's Park would ever be. Now sit back and relax, we'll soon be there.'

Far from relaxing, however, as Gareth negotiated the busy London traffic, Peggie knew that she was becoming

MAGGIE KINGSLEY   163

increasingly angry. He'd promised he would explain everything this afternoon and now he was taking her to meet his
mother instead. Well, if he thought this visit was going to
let him off the hook he was very sadly mistaken.

'This is it,' Gareth said when he finally stopped the car.

His home looked very much like any other small sub-
urban house, she decided as she followed him up the path.
And she immediately recognised the soft voice which
called, 'Gareth, darling, I didn't expect you back so soon.'

What she didn't expect, however, as Mrs Davies came
down the hall towards them was that Gareth's mother
would suddenly come to a halt with a startled gasp of dis-
tress when she realised her son was not alone. What she
didn't expect was to discover that Mrs Davies was quite
horrifically disfigured.

Gareth made tea but no one enjoyed it. Peggie did her
best to put his mother at her ease but the woman was
clearly deeply unhappy at her presence and when the clock
on the mantelpiece chimed four she got to her feet with
obvious relief.

'My mother always visits her friend on a Friday afternoon,' Gareth murmured when they heard the front door
close.

Peggie stared down into her empty cup and said nothing.

'Do you want any more tea?' he asked, reaching for the
teapot.

She shook her head.

'Well, aren't you going to say something?' he demanded.

She lifted her head slowly and stared at him. 'I would if
I could be sure that I could speak without losing my temper
first and hitting you,' she said with difficulty.

'Hitting me?' he echoed in confusion.

'That was a wicked thing to do,' she said, her anger
making her voice uneven. 'You should have told me.'

His lip curled. 'Don't you mean, warned you?'

'No, I do not mean warned me,' she cried. 'How dare you do that to your poor mother—springing me on her unannounced? Don't you have any feelings—any compassion at all?'

'Peggie—'

'This was a test, wasn't it—a test to see how I'd react?' she continued furiously. 'So how did I do in this little test of yours? Do I rate a B plus, or maybe a C minus for effort because I didn't run screaming out of the house and refuse ever to come back?'

'Every other woman who's met my mother has wanted to do just that,' he exclaimed, his face bitter.

'I am not "every other woman", Gareth, and I find it deeply insulting of you to assume that I am!' She clenched her hands together tightly and took a long shuddering breath to calm herself. 'How…how did it happen?'

'I got hold of a box of matches when I was four. I was shaking it like a rattle as so many kids do and the box suddenly ignited. My shirt caught fire and I was running around the kitchen, terrified, screaming, with my mother trying desperately to put out the flames, when she tripped over a can of kerosene and went up like a ball of fire.'

'And yet she survived.' She gasped.

He nodded, his lips slightly twisted. 'Oh, yes, she survived.'

'Gareth, it wasn't your fault—'

'She was such a beautiful woman,' he murmured as though she hadn't spoken, 'but afterwards she wouldn't go out, wouldn't see anybody. She used to love the farm but it became her prison.'

She crossed the room and knelt in front of him. 'People would have understood, Gareth. If she'd let them see her—'

'Allowed herself to be a sideshow, you mean?' he said harshly.

'No, not a sideshow,' she protested. 'Why must you always think the worst of people?'

His mouth tightened. 'Personal experience, I guess.'

She sat back on her heels and stared at him. 'You said your shirt went on fire. Were you burned too? Oh, Gareth, if that's why you think we could never have a future to-gether— Do you think what your body looks like would make a damn bit of difference to me?'

He gazed at her coolly, then got to his feet.

'You say it would make no difference,' he declared, be-ginning to unbutton his shirt. 'OK, Peggie. Let's see how much of a difference it would make.'

He pulled off his shirt and threw it to the floor and she had to bite down hard on her lips to stop the cry that sprang to them. His chest was every bit as broad as she'd imagined it would be but the skin that covered it had been horren-dously burned.

'Not sickened enough yet?' he asked, his mouth curving into a bitter smile as she stared at him. 'Then what about this?'

Slowly he undid the zip of his trousers and slipped them off, and then with one swift movement removed his boxer shorts and stood naked before her.

The burnt skin wasn't just confined to his chest but ex-tended all the way down his stomach and halfway down his thighs.

Hesitantly she got to her feet and even more hesitantly stretched out her hand to gently touch the lesions on his chest. He winced and closed his eyes but she didn't stop. She continued touching him until her fingers had traced all the ridges and twisted skin across his stomach and down his groin and onto his thighs.

'What…what treatment did you receive?' she asked, her voice professional, neutral, though inside she wanted to weep.

'Standard skin grafts.' He shrugged. 'As you can see they were extremely standard.'

'Gareth, I'm sorry—'

He knocked her hand away angrily. 'I don't want your pity.'

'I'm not offering any,' she flared. 'I was going to say I felt sorry for the pain you must have suffered.'

That he didn't believe her was plain. She could see it in his eyes, in the rigidity of his shoulders, in the set of his jaw.

'And this is why you think we can never ever have a future together?' she murmured.

'Isn't it obvious?' he retorted, reaching for his shirt.

'Not to me,' she cried, staying his hand. 'Gareth... Gareth, I love you. Not your body, not even your face— *you.*'

'Peggie, close your eyes.'

'W-what?' she stammered.

'Just do as I say, close your eyes.'

She did as he ordered and he clasped her hands to his chest. 'Now touch me again and tell me what you feel.'

'Gareth—'

'You can still feel them, can't you?' he said harshly. 'Even in the dark I can't forget I have this scarred body and neither would you.'

'Gareth...Gareth, do you love me?'

He stared down at her, his face a mixture of conflicting emotions, then reached for his trousers. 'What I feel isn't important,' he muttered. 'What I feel doesn't change anything.'

'It does!' she protested. 'Gareth, can't you believe me when I say it truly doesn't matter to me?'

'Marianne said it didn't matter,' he declared as he began buttoning his shirt. 'She was my SHO at Swansea Infirmary. We lived together for two years until she told me she couldn't stand the sight of my body any more.'

'Then she didn't love you.'

'And there was Julia who swore she loved me and yet

she would only let me make love to her in the dark until even the dark wasn't dark enough.'

'Gareth—'

'Peggie, you say now that it doesn't matter, but believe me I know that one day it would. I'm a plastic surgeon. Parents come to me every day wanting their children's disfigurements removed so that people won't shun them. I know how important appearance is.'

She was losing him, she knew she was. He was withdrawing from her, locking himself into a place she couldn't reach.

'Gareth, if I developed breast cancer,' she said quickly, 'if I had to have a radical mastectomy—would you find my body revolting?'

'Of course I wouldn't,' he said with irritation. 'Peggie, I know what you're trying to do but it's not the same.'

'It is,' she insisted. 'For a woman, losing her breasts would be like losing her proof of femininity.'

'That's ridiculous,' he exclaimed. 'A woman isn't a woman because she has breasts.'

'And a man's not a man because of the way his body looks,' she said softly.

He wanted to believe her. He truly wanted to believe her but he could not forget the look on Julia's and Marianne's faces when they'd left and he knew that if he ever saw it in Peggie's face it would destroy him.

'I'll take you home, Peggie,' he said.

'But, Gareth—'

'I'll take you home, Peggie.'

Chapter Ten

'OK, THIS is the operation schedule I've worked out for next week,' Gareth declared as he handed round the list, 'so if anybody would like to make any changes could they speak up now?'

'I was rather hoping to do Richard Sinclair's skin grafts on Monday, Gareth.' Tom frowned as he gazed down at the schedule. 'They've been in storage for ten days already and the longer I wait, the more chance there is he'll develop a Streptococcus pyogenes infection.'

'Peggie, how are you fixed for Monday afternoon?' Gareth asked, turning to her.

She shook her head. 'Solid appointments until five o'clock, I'm afraid.'

'And we've got Timmy Abuki's facial reconstruction after the removal of his tumour on Tuesday.' Gareth frowned. 'OK, we'll schedule Richard's grafts for Wednesday morning unless either of you have a problem with that?'

Tom and Peggie shook their heads.

'You do realise that you've given yourself no leeway at all on Thursday if any emergency comes in?' Tom observed, scanning the schedule again. 'With Angel's replacement not due to start for another ten days we could be in big trouble.'

'My Thursday morning clinics are usually pretty light,' Peggie said quickly. 'If it would be any help I could take on some of your cases, Tom—or yours, Gareth—'

'No,' Gareth said firmly. 'When you start sharing cases all that happens is you end up wasting half the consultation time familiarising yourself with the case notes.'

'It was just a suggestion,' she murmured.

'And a kindly meant one—' he nodded '—but it's not an option. We'll just have to hope no emergency comes in, and if it does play it by ear. OK, Tom, you'll have noticed I've put you down for Henry Yuill's toe replantation on Friday…'

Three weeks, Peggie thought as she watched Gareth discussing some point with Tom. It had been three weeks since Gareth had taken her to see his mother and nothing she had said or done had persuaded him that she didn't give a damn about his scarred body. She'd tried sweet reason, furious argument, even tears, but nothing had worked, and now the only subject he would discuss with her was work.

Patience, Peggie, she told herself as she saw him smile at something Sally said. He can't keep this up for ever. He can't shut you out of his life for ever.

But what if he does? her heart asked when they all stood up, the briefing for next week's operations at an end, and Gareth deliberately avoided making eye contact with her. What if he never believes you—what are you going to do then?

She refused to think about it—she refused even to contemplate it. He would come round. Somehow, some day, she would make him see sense, she was sure she would.

'Fancy a coffee, Peggie?' Sally asked, falling into step beside her as they came out of Gareth's consulting room.

Peggie glanced at her watch. 'I'd love one but I'm due in theatre in forty-five minutes to assist Tom with the last of Christopher North's skin grafts, and I've got masses of paperwork I really should tackle—'

'You take yours white with no sugar, don't you?' Sally observed, her eyes dancing, and Peggie chuckled.

'OK, you twisted my arm—just a quick one.'

'Did I tell you I met Angel last week in Oxford Street?' Sally continued as she led the way to the staff room. 'She looked like a ship in full sail and quite blissfully happy.'

'Her baby's due next month, isn't it?' Peggie observed

as Sally took two cups out of the cupboard and spooned some coffee into them.

'September fourteenth to be exact, though how in the world anyone can ever give a precise date is beyond me. Do you want a biscuit with your coffee or are you dieting again?'

Peggie gazed down into the tin Sally was holding out to her, hesitated for a second, then took two chocolate ones.

'I know, I know.' She laughed, seeing Sally's eyebrows rise. 'A second on the lips, a lifetime on the hips, but right now I feel like pigging out. Isn't Jack joining us for coffee?' she continued as she kicked off her shoes and curled up in one of the seats. 'He doesn't normally refuse a dose of caffeine.'

'He's in IC giving Fiona MacKenzie her medical before Gareth does her skin grafts tomorrow.'

'I bet Fiona's arrival in IC gave Christopher and Steven something to think about,' Peggie observed as Sally switched off the kettle. 'A partially severed foot must rate pretty high on the "yuck" stakes of those little ghouls' table of operations.'

Sally laughed. 'Steven's being discharged today, isn't he?'

Peggie nodded. 'He'll have to come back for more surgery, but being discharged is at least the first step on the road to recovery.'

'You must be looking forward to helping Gareth create a working hand for him?' Sally observed.

Gareth had said it would take him four to five years to give Steven a fully working hand again, Peggie remembered, accepting the coffee Sally was holding out to her. In five years' time she'd be thirty. In five years' time Angel and her husband would probably have had another baby, if not two. Would she still be working for Gareth at Lizzie's, still hoping he'd come round, still wishing he'd see that she loved him? It was an overwhelmingly depressing thought.

'How are things progressing between you and Jack?' she asked, deliberately changing the subject.

Sally smiled. 'It's early days yet, and he's still very insecure, but at the moment everything's OK.'

'I'm glad he told you the truth eventually,' Peggie murmured, sipping her coffee.

'So am I. Idiot man—as though something like that would make a damn bit of a difference to me. In fact, it's actually great being with a man who, when he makes love to you, is constantly asking what you like and what you don't like, and actually listens instead of wham bam, thank you, ma'am.'

'It must be.' Peggie sighed enviously.

Sally stared at her for a moment, then cleared her throat. 'Look, I'm really sorry about you and Gareth. It's hell when you fall in love with someone who doesn't love you back, but to fall in love with a man who's gay…'

Peggie groaned inwardly. Gareth had assured her he'd told Jack the truth about his sexuality but either he hadn't been very convincing or Jack hadn't been listening.

'Sally, I think you and I need to have a little talk,' she said firmly, and, taking a deep breath, she told the staff nurse everything. Every last and sorry detail.

'Oh, God, that's awful,' Sally exclaimed, tears shimmering in her eyes, when she'd finished. 'If I had that Marianne and Julia in this room, I'd…I'd…'

'Tear out their hair strand by strand, then get to work on their teeth as an encore?' Peggie smiled ruefully. 'I've thought of considerably worse things I'd like to do to them, believe me.'

'Can't you make him see that just because he's had some bad experiences with women it doesn't mean we're all the same?' Sally protested.

'I've tried, Sally, but it's like talking to a brick wall.'

'God, but men really can be pathetic at times, can't they?' the staff nurse declared irritably. 'It's like Jack—making such a big deal about his virginity. As though I cared—as though any halfway decent woman would care. Gareth's scars—are they…are they pretty bad?'

'Probably amongst the worst I've ever seen,' Peggie replied with a crooked smile.

'But you still love him,' Sally said softly.

'Oh, Sally, if only you knew how much,' Peggie murmured, her lips trembling.

'Then fight for him.'

'How? I've tried sweet reason, argument—'

'Seduce him.'

'Seduce…?' Peggie's jaw dropped, then she shook her head. 'Number one, I'm hardly the *femme fatale* type, and number two, it wouldn't change anything.'

'It would if somebody walked in on you,' Sally observed thoughtfully. 'Whatever else Gareth might be, he's the old-fashioned type—an honourable man.'

'You mean I should blackmail him into marrying me?' Peggie gasped. 'No way—never. Sally, what kind of marriage would that be, based on deceit?'

'But he loves you, doesn't he?' the girl protested. 'All you'd be doing is giving him a little bit of a nudge, and after you were married—'

'Forget it, Sally,' Peggie said firmly. 'If I wait—if I'm patient—he'll see reason eventually, I know he will.'

'But—'

'No, Sally,' she declared. 'My way is better, believe me. And now I really must go,' she continued as the staff nurse opened her mouth, clearly intending to protest. 'Tom might be tolerant about timekeeping but he's not a saint.'

The staff nurse meant well, Peggie knew she did as she headed off for the operating theatre, but not only was her idea morally wrong it was also laughable. How in the world could she ever seduce anyone? With her figure and looks, she'd have as much likelihood of success as a bikini sales-woman trying to sell her product to Eskimos.

'Cutting it a bit fine, aren't you?' Jack grinned when he saw her. 'Gareth's been drumming his heels for the last five minutes.'

'Gareth?' she gasped. 'But I thought Tom was doing Christopher's op?'

'Last-minute change of plan,' he replied. 'Which will teach you not to believe all you see in the operation sched-ules from now on.'

'Five minutes—that's all I'll need,' she replied, dashing into a changing cubicle. 'Just give me five minutes.'

'I'll tell him,' Jack called back, 'but it better be just five minutes, Peggie, or I wouldn't want to be in your shoes.'

Oh, wonderful, just wonderful, she thought, throwing off her clothes and dragging on her scrubs. If there was one thing Gareth couldn't stand it was unpunctuality. In fact, it was a standing joke in the unit that he probably wouldn't even consider death a sufficient excuse for lateness. He'd hang her out to dry, she knew he would.

But he didn't. All he said as she crept unobtrusively into the operating theatre was, 'Good, you're here now.'

Relief surged through her, but it was a relief that was destined to be short-lived. Every time she looked up during the operation his gaze was on her—thoughtful, pensive—but when their eyes met he looked away immediately. When she reached for the forceps or a scalpel she knew he was watching her, and when the operation was over and she emerged from her changing cubicle and began brushing her hair she could see in the mirror over the sink that he was watching her still.

Something was going on—she knew it was. For the last three weeks Gareth had studiously avoided looking at her at all and yet now... Now, it was almost as though he was trying to imprint the memory of her face on his mind and the thought worried her much more than his previous cool detachment ever had.

'Gareth—'

'Peggie—'

They'd spoken in unison and it was he who flushed, not her.

'I just wanted to say that Esther Black's coming in to see me this afternoon and as you assisted me with her cleft palate op I wondered if you'd like to see the results,' he said quickly.

'What time's her appointment?' she asked, balancing her handbag on the edge of the sink and extracting her diary from it.

'Four-thirty. She's my last patient.'

She frowned. 'I'd like to see her but it really depends on my clinic. If I can make it, I will.'

He nodded, but he didn't leave as she had expected—he simply stood where he was, his eyes on her.

She wished he would simply say what he wanted to say and get it over with. His constant scrutiny was making her edgy, uncomfortable, and nervously she reached for her handbag, only to let out a muttered exclamation as she sent it clattering to the floor.

Quickly she bent to retrieve it just as he did and their heads promptly collided.

'Oh, I—I'm sorry,' she stammered, momentarily seeing stars.

'I believe the last time this happened I said, "Not half as sorry as I am,"' he said ruefully, holding out her bag to her.

A smile curved her lips as she took it. 'And if I remember rightly, I think I said, "It's all right—I'm a doctor."'

He smiled back at her and her heart faltered as she realised he hadn't smiled at her like this since the night they'd made love.

He clearly realised it too and, though his smile faded, he didn't move away.

'Peggie...'

His voice was low, husky, sending faint tremors running down her back, and when he stretched out his hand and touched her hair gently she couldn't have said anything if her life had depended on it.

All she was conscious of was the rapid pulse-beat at his throat, his deep green eyes holding hers, and the knowledge that if she reached out she could touch him too as she'd been wanting to since that night in her flat.

'Gareth—'

'There's something important I'd like to discuss with you before you start your clinic this afternoon,' he declared, his voice suddenly neutral, completely professional as he swung abruptly away. 'Would two o'clock in my room be convenient?'

She knew her cheeks must be red—she could feel them burning—but she managed to reply with scarcely a tremor, 'Two o'clock's fine. Gareth—'

'Coming for lunch, Peggie?' Jack asked cheerily as he clattered into the changing room.

Boy, but the anaesthetist really did have the world's worst timing, she decided.

'I don't know, Jack. I—'

'Everybody's got to eat,' he interrupted.

Oh, yes, everybody had to eat, she thought, gazing after Gareth as he walked out of the changing room without so much as a backward glance, but everybody needed love too. Everybody needed to feel wanted, to be needed.

'Peggie?'

The anaesthetist's eyes were on her, curious, slightly concerned, and she forced a smile to her lips.

'Lunch sounds great,' she replied.

And she supposed it should have been. Jack kept up an amusing flow of stories about the staff at the hospital and she smiled and laughed in what she hoped were the right places, but all the time she thought about Gareth.

She knew now why he'd specialised in plastic surgery, why he was so good with children who were disfigured, and why he wouldn't let anyone get close to him. She knew so much about him apart from the one thing that really mattered—how to reach him, how to break down the barriers he had erected around himself.

Patience, Peggie, she told herself. Rome wasn't built in a day and one day he'll see you meant every word you said to him.

Yes, but when? her lonely heart asked. When?

She made sure she wasn't late for her appointment at two o'clock. In fact she arrived five minutes early just to be on the safe side.

'You did say there was something important you wanted to discuss with me,' she declared when he glanced up in surprise at her entrance.

He reached into the drawer of his desk and pulled out a letter. 'Not exactly discuss. I received this this morning and I thought you might find it interesting.'

Her heart sank with disappointment. They were always receiving invitations to seminars and conferences, and, interesting though they generally were, the last thing she wanted to do at the moment was head off to some three-day conference.

'What is it?' she said without enthusiasm.

'An ex-colleague of mine has written to tell me about a new experimental plastic surgery unit he's setting up in Edinburgh and when I read in the letter that he was looking for people to join his team I immediately thought of you. It's a wonderful opportunity, Peggie,' he continued as she stared at him silently. 'You'd be in at the start, able to make a positive and very real contribution, and some of the surgery he's planning is quite revolutionary.'

She glanced down at the sheet of paper in his hand, then up at him again. 'You said you immediately thought of me. Why not of Tom or Jack?'

'Because Tom has family commitments in London, and Jack... Well, Jack and Sally appear to be getting quite close whereas—'

'I have nothing to keep me in London,' she finished for him, her voice tight. 'I presume your ex-colleague didn't know of any units being set up in Aberdeen or Inverness?'

'Aberdeen or Inverness?' he echoed, puzzled.

'You must be quite disappointed that you can't send me any further from London than Edinburgh?'

A flash of anger appeared in his eyes for a second, then they were shuttered. 'You don't have to apply for the job, Peggie. All I'm saying is it would be a wonderful opportunity for you—a promotion, in fact.'

Of course it was a wonderful opportunity—an opportunity any other SHO would probably have killed for—and by offering it to her he was effectively promoting her right out of his life.

'So, do you want to read this or not?' he asked, his eyes fixed on her as he held out the letter.

What she wanted was to cram the letter down his throat until he choked on it. What she wanted was to grab him by the shoulders and pummel him senseless for being such a proud and stupid man, but she accepted it without a word and stuffed it into her handbag.

'Peggie, I know it's a daunting task to think of uprooting yourself so soon after you've just settled in London but it really would be for the best if you took this appointment,' he murmured.

'Best for who, Gareth?' she declared icily.

'Peggie—'

'I'll read it and let you know what I decide,' she interrupted, and walked briskly out of his room before the tears she could feel welling in her eyes had the chance to fall.

She was not going to cry. She was *not* going to cry. Don't get mad, get even, her mother always said. Well, if he so desperately wanted her out of his life, she would damn well oblige him. If he was so desperate to get rid of her that he was pulling in favours from ex-colleagues, she'd take the post in Edinburgh and to hell with him.

'Everything OK, Peggie?' Sally asked, looking up in surprise as she banged into her consulting room.

'Fine—couldn't be better,' she snapped. 'Could you send in my first patient, please?'

And although she did, Peggie was conscious all through the afternoon of the girl's gaze on her, anxious, concerned.

It seemed a long afternoon—it seemed an interminably long afternoon—and it was twenty to five by the time she'd seen her last patient. Go home, she urged to herself as she wearily got to her feet, but she really wanted to see Esther Black again and if that meant seeing Gareth too she'd just have to smile and bear it.

Slowly she walked along to his room but when she opened the door it wasn't the fact that the operation had clearly been a complete success that arrested her attention. It was the expression on Gareth's face as he gazed down at the little girl in his arms.

Never had she seen such an expression of tenderness on a man's face before and when their eyes met over the child's head her heart twisted inside her.

Taking the job in Edinburgh wouldn't solve anything. Taking the job would simply be cutting off her nose to spite her face. She loved him, she was always going to love him, and somehow—*somehow*—she had to make him see it before it was too late.

'Is Esther OK?' Sally asked when Peggie went back to her room after the interview with the Blacks was over.

'Yes…yes, she's fine,' Peggie murmured, picking up one of the files on her desk and putting it down again absently.

Sally looked at her uncertainly. 'Peggie—'

'What you said before about me seducing Gareth,' she interrupted. 'How would I do it?'

A wide smile lit up the staff nurse's face. 'Now you're talking! OK, Esther was his last patient today and he usually spends forty-five minutes or so on his files before he goes home, so that gives us half an hour to get you ready.'

'I didn't mean I was going to do it now,' Peggie protested. 'I only meant—'

'Thank goodness you're wearing your red dress,' Sally continued as though she hadn't spoken. 'It's his favourite.'

'Is it?' Peggie declared, momentarily diverted.

'Absolutely.' Sally nodded. 'I've noticed he can't keep his eyes off you whenever you wear it and we definitely want you to be alluring.'

'Alluring,' Peggie repeated, feeling anything but. 'Sally—'

'Now you go along to his room, sit down like this and cross your legs like so, making sure you're revealing a goodly amount of thigh. You haven't got any holes in your tights, have you?'

'No, I haven't, but—'

'Then you flutter your eyelashes and lean seductively over his desk.' Sally paused and frowned. 'It's a pity that dress of yours shows so little cleavage. Are those buttons down the front real or fake?'

'Real. Sally—Sally, what are you doing?' Peggie exclaimed as the girl leant forward and deliberately undid two. 'I can't go into Gareth's room with my dress half undone!'

'We're hoping it's going to be completely off before we're finished, you idiot,' Sally replied. 'Look, you've got terrific boobs,' she continued as Peggie stared at her in dismay, 'and if we give him a tantalising glimpse of them he'll be all over you in seconds.'

'Sally, I really don't think I can do this,' Peggie began uncertainly. 'I know you mean well, but—'

'Look, do you want Gareth or not?' the girl demanded.

'You know I do.'

'And have you got a better idea?'

Peggie had to admit she didn't.

'Supposing—just supposing—this plan of yours actually does work and he's all over me as you think he will be—what happens then?' she asked.

Sally frowned. 'Five minutes for you to cross your legs and flutter your eyelashes at him. Two minutes for you to lean seductively over the desk. OK, I'll come in without knocking after fifteen minutes and hopefully catch the pair of you in the act.'

'What if he doesn't find me alluring?' Peggie demanded. 'What if he locks the door—what if—?'

'Will you just go?' Sally insisted, pushing her firmly towards the door. 'It's a quarter to six. Don't think ''what ifs''—just do it!'

I'm insane, Peggie thought as she walked slowly down the corridor, completely insane. This is never going to work. At best Gareth's going to laugh at me, and at worst… At worst he's going to stare at me blankly and ask what the hell I'm doing.

She stopped and half turned to see Sally watching her.

'Go!' the staff nurse urged. 'If you want him, fight for him. If you don't you'll regret it for the rest of your life.'

She was right, she would, and with an effort Peggie straightened her back and without bothering to knock went straight into his room, but he wasn't sitting at his desk as she had expected. He was standing by the window, staring out.

'I thought I told you I didn't want to be disturbed, Marge,' he observed without turning round.

His tone was anything but encouraging and she moistened her dry lips and cleared her throat. 'It isn't Marge—it's me—Peggie.'

He turned round fast and for a split second his eyes flared

with something that made her cheeks burn. The look was gone in an instant, but it was enough. If you want him, fight for him, Sally had said. Well, she was going to do her damnedest.

'I thought you'd gone home?' he said harshly but she didn't answer. She simply sat down and crossed her legs as instructed. 'Is there something you want?' he continued, moving away from the window and sitting down behind his desk as though deliberately putting a barrier between them.

You, I want you, she wanted to say, but determinedly she fluttered her eyelashes instead.

He stared at her for a second, then frowned. 'Have you got something in your eye?'

'S-sorry?' she stammered.

'Your eye—you seem to have something in your eye. I have eye drops in my desk—'

'I don't need eye drops,' she retorted in exasperation, then bit her lip as he gazed at her with surprise.

She got to her feet and perched herself on the edge of his desk.

'Peggie, be careful with those papers—'

'Forget about the papers,' she murmured, leaning towards him and lowering her voice to what she hoped was a fair imitation of Frances Harper's sexy drawl.

It should have been provocative—it might well even have been provocative—if, as she leant forward even more, her elbow hadn't caught the vase of flowers on his desk and sent it flying.

'Hell and damnation, Peggie, my files!' he exclaimed, leaping to his feet as a cascade of cloudy green water slopped all over them.

'I'm sorry—I'm so sorry!' she cried, frantically attempting to mop up the water with the skirt of her dress only to be unceremoniously elbowed aside as streaks of red began to appear on the clinical notes.

'You're making it worse!' he protested. 'We need something white—'

'Your shirt,' she exclaimed. 'Your shirt's white.'

He tore it over his head without a second's thought, sending buttons flying everywhere.

'Of all the cack-handed, hare-brained... What in the world possessed you to sit on my desk in the first place?'

'Are the papers all right?' she asked, ignoring his question.

'Do they look all right?' he demanded.

She had to admit they didn't.

'Maybe Admin could send you another set, a duplicate?' she suggested uncomfortably.

'I suppose they could, but I'm hardly going to look very professional when I ask for one, am I?' he retorted.

She forbore from pointing out that he didn't look in the least professional at the moment, standing in the centre of his office naked from the waist up.

Much the same thought must have occurred to him because he suddenly reached into his filing cabinet and yanked out a shirt.

If he put it on the moment would be lost, and she knew there would never be another opportunity like this—an opportunity to show him once and for all that the scars on his body which glinted so cruelly under the fluorescent lighting really didn't matter to her.

Quickly she walked over to him and before he could move away she stood on her toes and lightly brushed his lips with her own.

'Don't do that,' he said, his voice suddenly hoarse.

'Why not?' she whispered, placing a kiss at the base of his throat.

He put out his hands to fend her off. 'Peggie, stop it.'

She grasped his wrists with her fingers. 'Why? Don't you like what I'm doing?'

'No!' he said with a strangled intake of breath as she leant forward and teased one of his nipples with her tongue.

'Liar,' she chuckled.

'Peggie, stop this at once.' He gasped when she ran her fingers lightly along the waistband of his trousers. 'You know it's hopeless. There's nothing I can offer you—'

'There's yourself, for a start,' she interrupted, placing a series of kisses along his collar-bone.

'I'd call that a very poor bargain,' he replied shakily.

'Gareth, I'm twenty-five—maybe I can't afford to be too choosy any more.'

A small smile curved his lips, then was gone. 'Peggie, look at me—really look at me—and you know there's a hell of a lot worse further down. You could do so much better than me.'

She nibbled his ear gently and then ran her tongue along his lower lip, teasing it. 'I know I could, Gareth, but, you see, the trouble is I've got such terrible, lousy taste.'

A deep throaty chuckle came from him. 'Peggie—'

'Mr Davies, what are you *doing!*'

He turned quickly, his cheeks scarlet, and Peggie buried her face in his shoulder to hide her laughter. Sally was standing in the doorway, her face a picture of outrage.

'Sally—Staff Nurse Cooper—believe me, it's not how it looks,' he exclaimed.

'You mean you're getting married?' She beamed.

'No, we are not getting— Oh, hell,' he declared as the phone rang. 'Look, don't move—either of you.'

'How come he's the one who's half undressed?' Sally hissed in an undertone as Gareth pulled on his shirt and went to answer the phone.

'Things went a bit awry,' Peggie muttered back.

'You can say that again,' Sally whispered, 'but, as they say in the old adage, "all is not lost". Mr Davies,' she continued when he put down the phone, 'when you say you're not getting married—'

'Now, look, Sally,' he interrupted, only to come to a halt. He glanced from her to Peggie, then a smile began to curve his lips, and suddenly he started to laugh—a deep-throated laugh of pure amusement that Peggie thought was the most wonderful sound she'd ever heard. 'This is a set-up, isn't it?'

'Of course it's not—'

'Sally, we might as well come clean,' Peggie broke in, her eyes fixed on Gareth, a half-smile on her lips. 'Yes, it's a set-up, Gareth.'

'I should tan your hide, Sally Cooper,' he declared, 'and as for you, Peggie O'Neill—'

'I don't want to hear this,' Sally said, putting her hands quickly over her ears. 'If you're into sadomasochism, Mr Davies—'

'Sadomasochism?' he repeated, his jaw dropping, then he pointed to the door. 'Out, Sally.'

'But—'

'*Out!*' he repeated in a tone that brooked no opposition and she went with a giggle. 'OK, confession time, Peggie,' he continued, turning to her when they were alone. 'Perhaps you'd like to tell me—what was that little performance all about?'

'Gareth—'

'Well?'

He was smiling and she flushed. 'I was…I was trying to seduce you.'

'And doing a pretty damn good job of it too.' He chuckled. 'What was Sally's next line going to be after she hopefully found you with your dress ripped off and your tights in tatters? ''Unhand that woman, you lecherous fiend—unless you're going to marry her, of course.'''

'Something like that,' she admitted.

'Peggie, listen—'

'No, you listen for a change,' she interrupted. 'Gareth, I love you—*all* of you. If my being here at Lizzie's makes you uncomfortable then I'll leave, but I won't take that job in Edinburgh. I'll stay on in London even if it means I have to stack supermarket shelves to live.'

'Peggie—'

'I won't give up on you. I'll hang about Lizzie's on my days off. I'll wear my skirts higher and higher, and my necklines lower and lower, until you have to pay attention to me.'

'Those two undone buttons on your dress are more than enough already, believe me,' he said huskily, coming closer to her. 'Peggie—'

'I know you don't believe me when I say that the scars on your body don't matter—'

'Peggie, I think you've just amply proved that they don't,' he said, putting his hands round her waist. 'Anyone who was prepared to do what you were trying to must mean what she says.'

'Then…?'

'Peggie O'Neill, you're the craziest girl I've ever met, but I do love you, and if you'll have me, I want to marry you.'

'You mean it?' she said, scanning his face uncertainly. 'You won't take it back later when you've had time to think, to reconsider?'

He strode to his door, threw it open, and roared at the top of his lungs, 'I have just asked Peggie O'Neill to marry me and I'm waiting to see if she'll say yes!'

For a second there was complete silence in the corridor, then Peggie heard the sound of running feet coming towards them.

'Well, Peggie?' Gareth said softly, holding out his arms to her. 'In about two seconds there's going to be enough witnesses out there to make sure I couldn't back out even if I wanted to. Will you marry me, because, as God is my witness, I love you and I want to marry you.'

She stared up at him tremulously, her throat so tight it hurt. 'Gareth—oh, Gareth, of course I will!'

And as he crushed her into his arms and kissed her long and hard, she didn't hear the yells of delight from staff clustered outside in the corridor. And as Gareth kicked the door shut and locked it she didn't hear any of their loud whoops of encouragement either. All she knew as he kissed her again was that she had never been more happy in all her life.

READER SERVICE™

The best romantic fiction direct to your door

Our guarantee to you...

The Reader Service involves you in no obligation
to purchase, and is truly a service to you!

There are many extra benefits including a free
monthly Newsletter with author interviews,
book previews and much more.

Your books are sent direct to your door
on 14 days no obligation home approval.

We offer huge discounts on selected books
exclusively for subscribers.

Plus, we have a dedicated Customer Care team
on hand to answer all your queries on
(UK) 020 8288 2888
(Ireland) 01 278 2062.

MILLS & BOON®

Makes any time special

Enjoy a romantic novel from
Mills & Boon®

Presents...™ *Enchanted*™ TEMPTATION®

Historical Romance™ ⊢↓MEDICAL ROMANCE®

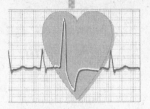

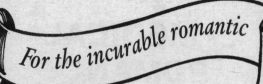

Historical Romance™

From Medieval pageantry to the Restoration and glittering Regency Seasons

1066 - 1920
all the ages of romance

Four new titles available every month

Available from

READER SERVICE™

The best romantic fiction direct to your door

on subscription